After Freud

After Freud

a novel by
MARY ELSIE ROBERTSON

State University of New York Press
ALBANY

Published by
State University of New York Press, Albany
© 1980 State University of New York
All rights reserved
Printed in the United States of America
No part of this book may be used or reproduced
in any manner whatsoever without written permission
except in the case of brief quotations embodied in
critical articles and reviews.
For information, address State University of New York
Press, State University Plaza, Albany, N.Y., 12246
Library of Congress Cataloging in Publication Data

Robertson, Mary Elsie, 1937-
    After Freud.

    I. Title.
PS3568.02497Af   813'.54   80-20497
ISBN 0-87395-462-9
ISBN 0-87395-464-5 (pbk.)

*With gratitude to the Yaddo Corporation, which gave me the time and conditions
to complete this book.*

10 9 8 7 6 5 4 3 2

For Peter

Prologue

"Do you want me to come with you?" Nina asked, hovering just inside the bedroom door. "I will if you want me to."

"I'd better do it myself," I said, unbuttoning the green shirt that I saw was too wrinkled to wear after all and throwing it onto the bed with the other discards. "If I do get in to see Walter maybe it would be better if he didn't have his wife *and* his mother to contend with. Both of us might be a little bit overpowering . . . and anyway . . . oh, look, Nina, what am I going to wear? Everything I've got looks wrong. I'd say this gray skirt but I've just noticed the hem's too short. It's an old skirt and I never let it out . . ."

I wanted to appear calm, sensible, a person to be depended on. The thing I didn't want was to dash in wildly into P-Wing — late — my blouse coming out of my skirt, my hair blown into my eyes, the most distraught looking woman in the building.

So I rummaged wildly through the heap of clothes on the bed like a dog looking for food among the garbage, until Nina held up a grey skirt and a white blouse and said with authority, "Wear that. And if you wear your black boots the skirt length won't be noticeable."

So with that stamp of approval I put on the skirt and blouse and decided it would do. Not that Nina can be relied on about clothes. She was standing at that moment in a long, striped caftan bought on her travels and with a raspberry shawl over her shoulders — a color which clashed terribly with the apricot and apple green of the caftan.

While I combed my hair, peering nearsightedly at the mirror, my hand suddenly started trembling.

"I feel so nervous about seeing Walter in that place. What if he's just sitting there like a turnip? Maybe he won't even know me. When I say 'Hello, Walter' what if he just goes on smiling out the window . . . I wouldn't know what to do."

"If Walter is like a turnip then they won't let you in to see him. Simple as that. Put on a touch of lipstick, now. You look so pale."

"Isn't that just the light in here?" I said, peering wildly into the mirror, but I put on a daub of pink lipstick anyway.

"Now," Nina said, straightening my shoulders with her hands, "Put a little starch in your backbone and you're off."

As I buttoned my coat I avoided looking in the mirror again. I didn't want to know if my boots were down at the heel and my coat scruffy around the collar. I didn't want harsh reality spoiling what little starch I was able to muster.

From the waiting room in P-Wing of the University Hospital, I could see Dr. Fassbinder coming down the corridor to get me—a short man with iron grey hair and stern expression, wearing a white coat a little long in the sleeves.

The coat and the serious expression made him just the psychiatrist, deeply involved in his work. He didn't look as friendly as he had the last time I saw him, at the Stacks' Christmas party. Or maybe it was the memory of that last terrible time we were together which filled me with such agitation that I hurried down the hallway beside him clutching one of the University Hospital's *Harpers* and had to run back to put it in a chair.

"Are we going straight down to Walter's room?" I asked as I caught up.

I was relieved when Dr. Fassbinder said that we were going to his office first, though I felt a little guilty about that relief. Dr. Fassbinder, however, seemed to have expected it.

"Most people are nervous when they visit here for the first time," he told me as he ushered me into his office. "It's perfectly natural you should feel apprehensive."

I sat uneasily on the edge of my chair, tense as a bow. "Is Walter, you know, the way he was the last time I saw him?"

"Noooo," Dr. Fassbinder hastened to reassure me, "but I think that perhaps I should warn you about something . . . not such an unusual occurrence as you might think. And one we can deal with. But you might well find it disturbing." He took his handkerchief from his pocket and wiped a speck from his glasses. "The thing is, you see, that Walter thinks he's dead."

"What do you mean he thinks he's dead?"I said in alarm.

"He walks, talks, eats, sleeps, but in spite of that evidence to the contrary Walter feels he's well, *dead*. It's a rather common delusion, believe me. And he may not say anything about it to you. But if he does ask if you smell something odd, or if he apologizes for having a cold hand, just turn the conversation into other channels."

"Oh my lord!"

Dr. Fassbinder leaned forward and fixed his eyes on mine in a way that he probably meant to be reassuring. "I don't mean to scare you. And you might not see anything unusual in the way Walter acts at all. Just remember to be yourself. Be natural."

I didn't ask how I was meant to achieve this since I knew, anyway, that there was no possible way I could be natural with Walter on this visit. What did Dr. Fassbinder expect of me? That I could ignore everything that had happened?

What he expected, immediately, was for me to follow him down the hallway to what he called the music room.

"Has Walter taken up the violin since I saw him last, then?" I asked, and laughed nervously to show that my question was facetious.

"The music room is where people go to listen to music, although there is a piano and people do sometimes play . . ."

Dr. Fassbinder avoided, I noticed, calling the inhabitants of P-Wing *patients*. They were all just people, going through heavy weather, perhaps, but no different from the rest of us.

When we got to the door of the music room I panicked. If Dr. Fassbinder hadn't been there, opening the door, smiling encouragingly, I would certainly have fled. It's strange the things we do just because someone else is there with us, looking expectant. Most people even managed to get to the guillotine or the hangman's noose on their own two feet.

I saw Walter, of course, the instant I came into the room,

standing by the windows and turning slowly from them as he heard the door open. Dr. Fassbinder slipped away to the other side of the room to look through music with some woman sitting on the piano bench, and I was left alone with him.

He looked all right, walking toward me from the windows, and I took ridiculous comfort from his old mouse colored corduroy pants that were sprung in the knees and the blue cotton shirt that I'd washed, dried and folded fifty times at least in our past life together. I felt immediate, giddy relief.

Only, when he was much nearer, I became doubtful. His face was puffy—it had gone out of shape the way color blurs on wet paper—and, yes, he had grown heftier. He was swelling out of his clothes. Already the buttons of his shirt were straining.

"Dear!" Walter said, opening his arms to enclose me in a clammy embrace—he seemed to exude a kind of fertile heat the way bread dough feels as it rises on the back of the stove.

"How are you, Walter?" I asked, stepping back.

"Very well, really very well. I'm eating well as you can see." And he put his hands against his sides like a woman easing a corset.

I followed him back to the window where we sat in two facing chairs, our knees practically touching. Quickly Walter leaned forward, captured my hand and held it in his, pressing his palm against mine. Though I tugged lightly to free it he held on and so I sat tensely, ill at ease, knowing that the way he held my hand in his was not the friendly gesture it might seem.

"The girls are fine," I told him, talking fast, "and Nina has come over and is staying with us, or did Dr. Fassbinder tell you? And of course she sends her love . . ."

"Lee," Walter said, smiling in a way I didn't like, looking at my hand held so tightly in his, "I still don't understand how you could have done it when you knew how important . . . how much I loved you. I just don't *see* . . . you must have known it would kill me. And it did, it did. Surely you could see that I was dying that night. The night, you know, when you told me . . ."

I gave a frantic look over my shoulder to Dr. Fassbinder but his back was to me. He'd seen nothing, and Walter only took a tighter grip on my hand, squeezing it closer.

x

"Look, Walter," I said, as reasonably as I could. "I didn't *kill* you, you know. How can you think you're dead? You've actually grown more substantial since you've been here. And a ghost doesn't put on weight . . ."

"I guess I should know what my state is," Walter said, cocking his head a little so he could see my face. "I know now it's perfectly possible to be dead and still eat and walk around. Even," he looked at my pointedly, "talk to my wife. My best friend in the world."

I gave him a sharp look but could tell nothing. His face had puffed into a full moon, his eyes grown smaller. Where was the Walter I knew? This one was certainly not him.

"They must feed you very well," I said awkwardly, trying to take Dr. Fassbinder's advice and change the subject. "Haven't you gained a little weight?"

Walter rubbed my hand between his, back and forth, up and down, as though he intended skinning it. "I know you have a horror of my getting fat again. You wouldn't like me fat, would you? But it's only the swelling. You know that dead bodies always bloat."

"Cut that out!" I told him, suddenly losing my temper. "You know perfectly well you aren't dead so stop this stupid pretending. If I pinched you, you'd feel it all right. So how can a dead person feel?"

Walter rubbed his finger gently over my knuckles in that way he'd done so many times on nights when we held hands across the expanse of sheet and his eyes became, for a moment, Walter's eyes, as sad as a child who has been wrongfully slapped. "We had so much, Lee," he said. "And I don't understand why you wanted to ruin it."

A little later, in his office, while Dr. Fassbinder walked slowly up and down, his hands clasped behind his back, I pressed my teeth into my lip and tried not to cry.

"Will Walter ever be the way he was or is he going to be like this for good? Some fat man who hates me. Is that the way it's going to be?"

Dr. Fassbinder only shook his head doubtfully. "I'm afraid I'm not the Delphic Oracle," he said.

Not until Nina and I had gotten through supper, given Isabel and Felicity their baths and gotten them to bed, did we have a chance to talk, sitting in front of the fire, Nina with her embroidery, the colored floss laid out in orderly rows across the coffee table.

I found it hard to think of Nina as a mother-in-law because most people seem to have only bad things to say about mothers-in-law. And I love Nina. Now that my own mother is dead, killed along with my father in a car wreck the year before Isabel was born, Nina has become more than ever important to me. Not that I've seen much of her the last few years. Since Leon died — three years ago now — Nina has spent most of her time traveling. Greece, Morocco, the Canary Islands — she's seen them all. "Everytime I pass a cemetery I just kick up my heels a little higher," she's fond of saying. But Walter's breakdown brought her back to the heart of a New York winter from a Sicilian drizzle.

Walter and Nina don't look much alike. But as we sat there in front of the fire, I did suddenly see one resemblance after all — a look of guileless sweetness. Or at least Walter used to have a guileless sweetness.

And Walter is more staid than Nina; *he* would never traipse all over the world that way. That is about the last thing Walter would ever do.

"She sure is a case, isn't she?" was what my mother always said about Nina. She used to shake her head over Nina but she admired her all the same — both Southerners but of different kinds. Mother's family strayed into the foothills of the Ozarks, raising nearly every bite they ate, making their own soap and washing their clothes with it on a rub board. Nina's family came from England before the Revolution, bringing its silver and china with it.

Nevertheless, it was Mother and not Nina who insisted on wearing, one afternoon when I took her to Nina's house in Boston for a visit — hat, gloves, and shoes that matched her handbag impeccably. "Now I know what to wear and I'm going to wear it," she said to me, mildly annoyed when I said that the hat, at least, wasn't necessary. "I grew up in the hills and I'm proud of it, but that doesn't mean, now, that I have to go around wearing flour sacks, does it?"

Nina, who met us in her old gardening brogans, was the one who would have gotten a kick out of wearing flour sacks, and Mother knew it. They were both women of independent spirit and they recognized their similarities within five minutes of meeting. It didn't surprise me that Walter and I who had so much in common in spite of the differences in our backgrounds should have mothers who would get along too.

As we sat in front of the fire and Nina snipped off lengths of thread neatly with her embroidery scissors, I told her about my visit with Walter.

"Well, for heaven's sake," Nina said when I'd finished. "What a very peculiar thing to get into his head. If he were my age he wouldn't want to imagine himself a corpse. Time enough for all that is the way I look at it. It's such an extravagant notion. But Walter always did go overboard. When he was just a little boy he used to drive me wild the way he would hover so. Such a little busybody. He'd have followed me straight into the bathroom if he could have. Drove me absolutely wild at times. Though he was so sweet and loving."

"I know something about Walter's hovering."

Nina gave me a sympathetic look. "I'm sure you do, dear. He's a sweet man, Walter, not a bit like his father I don't think . . . you couldn't call Leon sweet, could you, whatever else . . . but my goodness even Walter would be a trial to live with. Any man is."

Leon, I was sure, had been a terrible man to live with. A paranoid who managed to lead a productive and lucrative life as the officer in a Boston bank, and who kept a pistol in his bedside table in order to shoot Nina's lovers if he ever found one.

For awhile he even had her followed by a private detective, a sad looking man with a permanently swollen red nose who used to slide down behind the dashboard of his dun colored Ford when Nina came out of the bakery with a loaf of French bread or out the door of St. Luke's Hospital where she went to roll bandages for cancer patients on Thursday afternoons. She got used to the detective — hovering around like a guardian angel — and missed him when he was eventually dismissed his surveillance. But then Nina was always above such details of living. She went on her round of good works, visiting her friends in old people's homes and lunatic asylums, taking Leon's suits to the cleaners and cooking the salt free foods he required because of his high blood pressure.

"Do you want to know something funny?" Nina said, measuring off a long strand of blue thread and snipping it off.

She looked up at me quizzically and a little mischievously like a child who is on the point of saying something he knows to be naughty.

"Well," Nina said, holding her needle up to the light and nudging it with her thread, "you know that tale, I'm sure, of when Leon had me followed by that detective — that odd little man who had a perpetual cold. I'm sure Walter's told you about that."

I nodded my head.

"But what Walter didn't tell you, because he couldn't have known, was that although Leon had no reason to have me followed when he did, what he succeeded in doing was in putting the idea in my head."

I must have looked blank because Nina laughed, her birdlike laugh, and shook her head.

"Why, there *was* a man I loved," Nina said. "And I've never told another soul. If you were my daughter I'd probably keep my mouth shut, but we don't have all the ancient wrongs hanging over our heads. I never spanked your little bottom when you were two, did I? And I've always felt of you as a special kind of daughter . . ."

"I've always felt specially about you, too, Nina."

"Well, then," she said, leaning back in her chair, "that was why I wanted to tell you about Otto. My friend." And Nina suddenly blushed, the wave of pink going up her cheeks to her forehead. "Isn't it ridiculous? And now I'm an old woman and Otto's dead, poor man. He died before Leon did in a silly accident. He went back home to Switzerland for a visit one summer and a cablecar rope broke, spilling him down one of the Alps. Hadn't been back in thirty-five years. And just tell me why that cablecar had to choose that moment to break? It must have been fate mustn't it?"

"Oh how sad, Nina," I said, taking her hand. We have so much in common after all. "But who was he and how did you get to know him?"

"Well, he was a clock repairer. A real craftsman. The best in Boston at repairing old clocks, and of course there are a lot of fine old clocks in Boston. A lot of fine, *broken* old clocks. We had a good many in our house. Luckily as it happened. Because that gave me the excuse, you see. We must have had ten clocks in the house and I took them all in the course of time to Otto. Then when we ran out of clocks we started on watches, so you see the excuse was so easy. Ready-made. And Leon, you know Leon, he loved to have everything well taken care of. He was so pleased that I was getting all the clocks seen to, all of them chiming together so sweetly on the hours."

"But how did you and Otto know? How did it develop, I mean?"

"That was the oddest and simplest thing. I took a clock to him one afternoon — a traveling clock as it happened. He was in the back with a magnifying glass over one eye — you know those things clock repairmen wear — and he came from the back with that thing flipped above his glasses. He just came out and said 'Yes? How can I help you?' And that was it. That was all. We looked at each other, we stood like two idiots I suppose, staring, and it was obvious . . . I mean we both knew right then what it was he could do for me. And what I could do for him too. And that's the tale. The start of the tale. It went on — would you believe it? — for ten years. Until he made that trip to Switzerland."

"And Walter never knew?"

Nina shook her head.

Poor Walter, betrayed by his mother, too.

I felt, when Nina fell silent, that she had read my mind.

"Oh, Nina," I said, "there's something I must tell you, too. Something I was putting off, something I didn't think you'd understand. And I don't even know where to start . . ."

"Start anywhere you like," Nina said, picking up her embroidery again. "There aren't any men in the house to shout at us to come up to bed. A houseful of women can do what we like, can't we?"

1

The obvious place to start is that September day when I took my first step into temptation — that fine day tinged with the melancholy of diminishing light.

On this day, as on all others, it's hard for Walter to say goodbye.

"Bye, Walter, have a good day," I call out cheerfully from the kitchen.

How Walter loves to linger, to hold onto the moment. He hangs around by the coat closet, fingering through jackets. "Will it rain do you think?" he says. "Should I wear my raincoat or will my corduroy jacket be enough?"

He depends on me, because I love him and know practically everything he's thinking, to get him through this hard transition of shutting the door behind him and going off into the dangerous world. So I crane my head to look out the kitchen window but all I can see between geranium leaves is bright blue sky. "Your jacket will be fine," I say firmly.

He sighs.

He loves it when the weather is uncertain and he can spend ten minutes going back and forth between the window and the closet.

"All right," he says finally, regretfully, putting his head in the kitchen doorway. "I'm off, then."

Felicity and Isabel, sitting at the table trying to empty their milk into each other's glass, are too busy to answer.

"Be good, dearlings," Walter says, bending down to kiss the tops of their heads. He shuts his eyes to savor the touch of their smooth hair on his lips.

I think that Walter carries around a picture always in his head, like a miniature a Victorian woman might have worn close to her heart in a brooch. There he is lying bloody in the middle of the road after some awful accident but tormented less by his battered body than he is by a terrible thought. He did not tell us all goodbye on that fateful morning — he left in a great hurry without a word or a kiss — and we will have to get through the rest of our lives with that to contend with.

"You know I love you, don't you?" Walter says every night before we go to sleep and every night I say yes, I love you too, Walter.

"Girls, drink your milk," I say sharply. "Walter, I'll see you late this afternoon same as always."

The time has come and Walter knows it. He comes to the sink and kisses me on the cheek.

"Be sure to get that tire checked," he says. "Don't drive faster than thirty on it in the meantime."

I always tell Walter I'll take care of whatever it is he's worrying about but I don't do it. I'm incapable of keeping up with the details.

But no detail is too insignificant for Walter to worry endlessly about. He broods over us like the Holy Ghost in that poem of Hopkins' — the Holy Ghost with a breast as warm as a setting hen's.

I hear the front door open but I have to wait quite awhile for it to shut. When it does there's reproach in the sound. I won't be standing in the doorway this morning, seeing him off, the pattern he likes best is broken, and any number of dangers can slip through the broken place.

As soon as the door closes, as softly as a sigh, I start shouting orders. "Shoes," I say to the girls. "Where're your shoes?"

Naturally they don't know.

I have to run around frantically retrieving one from the pots and pans drawer under the stove and another from the window sill on the stair landing. The one in the dog's bed is easy. Patsy sleeps with one every night as a comfort left over from his puppyhood. The fourth, though, the fourth. I know I've seen a shoe in some strange place but I can't think where. It's not in any place as obvious as under the sofa or lying in the middle of our bed.

2

"Where is it?" I ask Isabel finally. "Where's your damn shoe, Isabel?"

Isabel shakes her head slowly back and forth biting on her lower lip, but I can tell by the sly look in her eye that she knows perfectly well where it is only she won't tell. At three and three quarters she knows exactly, precisely, how to drive me frantic.

"All right," I tell her finally. "You can hop around on one foot all day for all I care. We're going."

Isabel starts making a peculiar noise, the one she always makes when she's really upset. A kind of keening. She holds her elbows in her hands, shuts her eyes tight, and rocks back and forth making this eery noise like one of the Trojan women mourning the dead.

She knows I'm capable of sending her off on one foot, and she's right. I'm already heading for the medicine cabinet to find the gauze so I can wrap it around her foot and tell her nursery school teacher she stepped on a tack, but Patsy turns over the garbage pail in the kitchen and there comes Isabel's shoe rolling across the floor. So that was the odd place I'd seen it.

"What was your shoe doing in the garbage, anyway, Isabel?" I demand as I buckle.

"Nobody else is wearing sandals now," Isabel says, sniveling but still managing to be accusing. "Everybody else has shoes."

"It's only October. I fail to see what's wrong with wearing sandals in October."

"Everybody else has shoes," Isabel says tragically, "and our feet get cold."

"You're lucky to have feet," I say as I hurry them out to the car. "Some people don't."

The girls ignore these little homilies of mine. They climb in the back seat of the car and crouch on their knees in a way that would give Walter fits. He always makes them sit straight and wear seat belts. But I don't feel like going through that hassle today and anyway I'm a fatalist. If we all get killed we get killed. I don't have as much reliance on order and forethought as Walter does. I have no delusion that I can stave off destruction singlehanded.

3

Maybe that's why I'm careless about details. There's no way I can cope with all the possibilities, all of the things there are to think about. Some people may imagine life as some orderly stream that they can navigate perfectly pleasantly by alternating crawl with backfloat, the nasty eddies and currents no danger if you see them up there and take measure. But I flail wildly, carried willy-nilly, dunked often, too swamped by the moment to take precautions about even obvious dangers that may lie up ahead.

When Isabel was a baby and I got her, with great difficulty, to one of those well baby checkups, the pediatrician picked up Isabel's hand as though it were a fish that had gone off and pointed to it accusingly. Exhibit number one. "Mrs. MacDougal," he said with great disdain in his voice, "cutting your baby's fingernails should be part of your routine, wouldn't you agree? A baby, you should keep in mind, is a totally helpless creature."

There were Isabel's fingernails looking like some Chinese mandarin's. I had somehow never noticed them before.

"But she isn't dirty," I said, wanting to get credit for something. "And look! She's so fat and she laughs all the time."

That sharp nosed pediatrician had no idea how hard it had been for me to get Isabel there on time, clean and wearing clothes that weren't even stained with sweet potato or orange juice, her hair brushed. And to have the whole thing go to waste because of fingernails.

"Goodbye, darlings," I tell the girls now as I let them out to run up the pretty flagged walk to the Rye Street Montessori School. Other mothers see their offspring to the door but I only watch mine, my toe tapping gently on the gas pedal, ready to race away. I see, when they're practically to the door, that I'm sending them off with their hair uncombed and with Felicity's jacket buttoned crookedly, but it's too late now. I just hope that Mrs. Faraday will think they got caught in a great gust of wind as they were coming in the door.

This is Felicity's first year in nursery school—children have to be toilet trained before Mrs. Faraday will take them on and Felicity, at two and a half, has made the grade. So for four hours, until 1:00 o'clock, I can go back home to my study at the top of the house, where only the tops of the skinny firs are visible from the windows, and try to work on what I call my autobiography.

"Autobiography?" Walter said, the first time I mentioned it back in August. "But you're only thirty. Don't you think you should wait awhile?"

But I told him I didn't mean one of those autobiographies where you write about all the exciting things that have happened to you and all the famous people you've known. The kind of autobiography I meant was one where you try to understand your life. How can I do anything with the rest of it if I don't understand what's gone on before?

Walter still looked confused and I reminded him of the story of Jake, one of his colleagues, who'd been passed over yet again for tenure. And when he went to the head of the department and asked why? Why should he be singled out in this way, the chairman had told him that it was because he hadn't lived up to his early promise.

"Remember how upset I got?" I reminded Walter. "Don't you think that's the most awful story? It's haunted me ever since."

"Oh, it is a terrible thing to say to anybody but, darling, it doesn't apply . . ."

"Oh yes it does," I said, starting to cry. "What's happened to my early promise I'd like to know? I can't make any sense . . ."

"Nothing, nothing's happened to your early promise," Walter said in anguish, pulling me down in his lap and rocking me like a baby. "I can't stand to hear you say that. It'll all be fine, I promise. With both girls in nursery school things will be different. I know they will. You'll see."

I wiped my nose on the back on my hand and told him I guessed so since I couldn't stand for him to worry, but I had doubts. Grave doubts. I'd had some power—a power like a magic wand—that somehow or other I had lost, that I was bereft of.

But I would try.

I started my autobiography with birth and so far I haven't gotten past it. I don't like my study at the top of the house where the fir trees groan and the light is obstructed by the overhanging roof. So there I am, day by day, dangling by my heels in the oily light of the decrepit little hospital in Kellam, Arkansas, hanging like a pear from a branch. I doodle on the paper. I make grocery lists. I want to run away.

Walter was intrigued when I told him I'd started with birth since he hasn't gotten back nearly that far with Dr. Fassbinder in the three years he's been making a pilgrimage three times a week up to his office in the medical college on the hill. Nowhere near that far back.

I'm mulling all this as I suddenly remember that I'm out of cheap typing paper and should make a stop at Simmons Stationery to buy some. I am — I admit it — pleased to find some excuse to keep me from my dark little room awhile longer.

It is, I've noticed before, at these moments when we're unprepared that the unexpected happens.

I have my hand on two packages of Prospect paper, am eyeing the Bic pens, when I feel an arm around my shoulders, the warm softness of wool, and look up to see Victor Smargorinsky's face, sharp, thin and intent, looking down at me.

Immediately I drop the paper on the floor and we both scramble around trying to pick it up. Though I've known Victor since Walter and I first came to Hanover and he is the husband (was the husband, I don't know what applies anymore) of one of my best friends, Victor has always had that effect on me. Everytime Victor looks at me at a party I blush, stumble, have this instant image of disaster. I'm certain I'm standing there by the punch bowl smiling with a piece of spinach from the dip caught between my front teeth. Or that my eyeshadow has smeared onto my cheek or that I've splashed suspicious looking drops of wine down the front of my dress. There's a kind of odd light in the back of his eyes which appears to record everything. Or I think that's what it is; it may be something else. I've always been self-conscious in Victor's presence though not because he's the chairman of Walter's department — art history — or the fact that he's probably the world expert on an obscure Florentine painter of the Renaissance named Jacopo Bernini. I'm not impressed by things like that. No, the reasons that impel me to instantly drop both packages of Prospect paper in Victor's presence lie elsewhere.

I've only seen Victor once since early May when Olivia — his

6

wife of eighteen years—ran off to live with an archaeologist in Rome. All summer Victor has been at Racquette Lake presumably licking his wounds, though his wounds, I see, are not altogether healed. At least the lines at the corners of his mouth have grown deeper and his eyes have red in the corners. But that old sharp intensity, like the tenseness of a hunting dog on the trail, is intact.

"Lee!" he says now, putting the Prospect paper firmly into my hands and fixing me with those curiously light eyes of his—a golden color like the eyes of wolves and some cats. "Would you believe it? You are the very person I wanted to see. I had your face right there, in the back of my mind, and suddenly there you were appearing before me. Perhaps I drew you here magically."

As he is talking he has taken my elbow and is propelling me to the cash register; if I don't pay quickly I feel that his long fingers, deft as a monkey's, will delve into my purse and pull out a palmful of change.

"You will come with me to Hessler's for a cup of coffee, won't you?" he says, even as he is nudging me, one hand cupping my elbow, to the door.

I don't say yes or no but am impelled across the street anyway. I steal glances at Victor's face as we dodge bicycles and cars but he has his eye out only for the dangers we may encounter; he is concentrating only on straining forward, as keen as a dog on scent.

The first year that Walter taught at the university we rented a house next door to Victor and Olivia. They were older and more experienced than we were and they enjoyed taking us under their wing—when we first knew them Olivia was thirty-nine and Victor forty-four. I was twenty-five and Walter twenty-nine and we had just gotten married.

Of course I was drawn to Olivia because she was colorful in all the ways I felt myself to be drab. Like a lot of Southerners—having grown up surrounded by fair skin and blue eyes—I was a sucker for olive skin and brown eyes, and Olivia looked like a gypsy. I suppose, come to think of it, that so did Victor, or at least he had the sharp, intent face that I associate with a doomed race.

It's harder for me to say why Olivia was drawn to me. Certainly there was nothing very prepossessing about me that first year at Hanover, sitting around on a sofa at parties holding hands with Walter — me in a neat little Peter Pan collar buttoned at the throat and Walter in a shirt too short in the sleeves as though we were twins dressed by some frugal mother.

But it was this very peculiarity that drew Olivia to me like a needle to a magnet, as I was afterwards to realize. I was, in Olivia's eyes, the writer from the Arkansas backwoods with a face out of a Walker Evans' photograph who would make my mark one day. What she thought of as my earthy background (she probably thought I had spent my childhood going around sticking pigs and making soap out of their fat) and my perceptiveness as a writer made her convinced that I knew far more than I did. She seemed to think I actually knew the answers to the questions she threw out at me as I sat on a stool in her kitchen watching her cook dinner: Did I think that life was essentially tragic? Did I think that a marvelous sex life was necessary for the health of the psyche? Did I think it had been a mistake to raise Kate (her daughter by her first husband — a man who died of a bee sting when they'd only been married a year) as an only child?

I was aware of Victor's presence in the house on these occasions though I seldom saw him. Sometimes he opened the door of his study and called to Olivia, "Could I trouble you for some iced coffee?" and once, in a peevish voice, "Have you seen the keys to my little file cabinet? I know you've done something with them, Livia."

Olivia shrugged her shoulders at these interruptions, raising her eyebrows in my direction as though she were sending me a message I would be sure to understand, but she got him his coffee, she found him his keys.

When Kate, his stepdaughter, was at home, Victor came out of his study, leaned against the mantle, and watched her work on her Latin. Their voices, excited and teasing, reached all the way to the kitchen and Olivia would frown in a way not very agreeable and say, "Those two." Sometimes I saw Victor and Kate walking to town together, hand in hand, swinging their arms the way high school sweethearts used to walk. I thought it was sweet the way they were so close.

8

It was the year that Kate went away to Swarthmore that I noticed some strain between Victor and Olivia. It started, or appeared to, over a graduate student of Victor's — a girl named Sherry — whom Victor hired to do some typing.

Since he did a lot of his work at home, Sherry would often let herself in the side door and slip into Victor's office without a word to Olivia. "She's only shy," Victor assured Olivia. "She's a hard worker, a good girl, Livia, really. You should be more tolerant of the poor child."

"Child!" Olivia said, her lip curling. "Maybe you need glasses, Victor dear. It's not very childlike the way she stares at you like a love sick spaniel. Sherry! Why not Mint Julip or Chablis?"

"If I didn't know better, Olivia, I would say you were jealous of that poor kid. And you know there's no reason, not the slightest, why you should be."

"I know, I know. She's just a poor girl, working her way through college, putting her eyes out over your illegible scrawl, a sweet, patient little thing who would gladly permit herself to be killed on your Chippendale desk, offering herself like a maiden to an Aztec god if it would do you any good, if it would spare your precious work or your precious face so lined with suffering — I know."

"Oh, for heaven's sake," Victor said, turning on his heels and walking indignantly from the room.

When he'd gone Olivia pounded her palm against her forehead. "Oh, I always go too far, damn it! But I know Victor's attracted to that silly little girl. The thing is, you see," she said cryptically, "he misses Kate so much. Let me tell you, Lee, it's a burden, an absolute burden to know more about someone than they know about themselves. It's so damn wearing. I know perfectly well that Victor's going to lift his nose out of the pages of Jacopo Bernini one of these days, blink in the light, and find some woman ten or twenty years younger than I am. The thing about Victor is that he's so mushy. Just like a pineapple somebody's left lying around too long."

But as it happened Olivia was the one to defect; she was the one who found her archaeologist in Rome the next year when

9

Victor was on sabbatical. I guess he was no mushy pineapple, having instead the bracing acidity of underripeness.

Victor and I slide into one of the highbacked booths in Hessler's and Victor orders coffee for both of us.

"Well," he says, leaning across the table, his eyes looking intently into mine. "How's your life, Lee?"

"Oh fine, fine," I say, chipping away at a little crack on the table with my fingernail. "How're things with you?"

"Things with me aren't so good. Pretty bad, in fact. Hell, Lee, I miss Olivia. I know I shouldn't admit it but you were a friend of hers. I can say that to you, can't I? Though lord knows I don't want everyone giving significant smiles behind my back, 'Oh, poor Victor is just torn apart. Did you know? Absolutely devastated. And did you hear that she just left him a *note* when she left? Tucked under the sugar bowl so I hear.' Oh god, Lee, I *hate* this town."

"I'm sorry," I say awkwardly, shuffling my feet under the table. "I really *am*, Victor."

I hear that solemn, lachrymose note in my voice—all wrong, wrong—but I have a talent for making the wrong response, or the inadequate response. It's not that I don't *know* what's needed but what comes out is wrong—it's like hearing musical notes in your head—true and in perfect pitch—which comes out your mouth like a chicken's squawk.

Victor brushes his hand across the table and puts, for a moment, his hand over mine. We are, I see, instant conspirators, two people given a sudden, unexpected bond.

"What do you hear from her?" he asks, his voice so low he's practically whispering. "Do you hear anything? Lord, I hope she's having a terrible time but I'll bet you're going to tell me she isn't."

"I haven't heard too much. Postcards and stuff."

"And what can you say on a postcard, right? A postcard is a non-message, a way of saying hello when you don't want to commit yourself. I'll bet if she were as happy as she thought she was going to be she'd write long estatic letters. She'd tell you all about the full moon shining on the ancient stones of the Coliseum and about

10

eating *gelati* on the Spanish Steps with Paolo or whatever his name is."

I can see that his words have cheered him up, and I don't want to disappoint him. I keep to myself the words of the last letter I had from her: "This may sound absurd to you, Lee—after all I'm a woman of forty-four (although that doesn't seem so old to me) but I'm in love as I haven't been since I was twenty. I'm obsessed, crazy, out of my mind—darling, I'm *wild* about Paolo! He has the most beautiful hands, so long and brown and sensitive, and his mouth! Those dimples at the corners like a satyr . . ."

Victor swallows his last bit of coffee, pushes the cup out of the way, and stands up. "Since I've already made a fool of myself, Lee, I might as well show you my next folly. You'll hear about it soon enough, anyway."

"I really ought to get back home . . . I was planning to work . . ."

"I know, I know, but indulge me just a little more, Lee. Consider me a helpless lunatic. I've just put a down payment on a rotting farmhouse six miles out in the country and I want someone to tell me that I haven't lost my mind. It won't take too long, I promise you."

So I say I'll come; I'm easily dissuaded from my dark little room, and anyway I'm flattered that Victor should single me out this way.

Our only other time of real intimacy was last May at Dean Stack's end of the term bash. Olivia had just left Victor, it was the beginning of the summer, and everyone was in his cups.

I happened to be hiding out in the hallway licking my wounds avoiding a supercilious man who'd just been brought in as a star in the English Department, a Faulkner expert from New Hampshire.

Liquor, when it does anything for me, makes me aggressive, and I had taken a dislike to the Faulkner expert on sight. "A new Englander could never really understand Faulkner," I informed him in a loud voice, leaning across the hors d'oeuvres to deliver this announcement.

11

"Yale University Press disagrees with you," the star said pompously. He had a long, unctuous face like an undertaker's. "They've published two volumes of my Faulkner criticism and I have a third in the works."

The star disliked me as much as I did him. "And what do you do?" he said, curling his teeth over his lip like a dog. "Or are you too busy taking care of children to do anything?"

"I write," I said quickly, though I knew what would follow. And it did. The star raised his eyebrows and the corners of his mouth drew back in a faint smile. I knew what he was thinking—oh, all you scribbling housewives, writing masturbatory fantasies and pretending you're making literature. And you have the audacity to tell me I couldn't know anything about Faulkner.

"And what do you write?"

"Short stories mostly."

I saw the debate in his eyes. Should he ask next the question about the novel or the one about publication?

He plumped for publication.

"Published anything?"

He thought he had me, I could see the gloat in the back of his eyes.

"Yes," I said, glad to be able to deliver that blow, puny as it was. Knew, too, that my answer would only stave off defeat for a moment.

"Where?"

"Oh, here and there. *Prairie Schooner, Georgia Review,* a little magazine called *Blue Moon* which is now defunct I think. Places like that."

No need to say that that *is* it. But the star knows anyway. I wouldn't have mentioned *Blue Moon* if I'd had any better place to mention.

"The world is full of would-be writers trying to get ditties in those little magazines," the star answered, and went off to find the paté.

So I was in the hallway wishing I were dead when Victor came through, holding his drink in his hand as though it were a candle, and looking pretty sad himself.

"Why do you look so downcast?" he said, catching me in the crook of his arm and pulling me against his chest.

"No reason. Except I wish I was dead."

"Oh, so do I," he said, patting my hair awkwardly with the hand holding the drink. "I wish I were dead and in my grave but what's the matter with you?"

We were both pretty drunk, swaying together there in the hallway while Victor sloshed his Scotch into my hair.

"I don't know, I don't know," I said, my tears soaking into the fine wool of Victor's jacket.

"Lee, Lee," he said, "what you need . . ."

But the sentence was never completed. A throng of other people pushed into our hallway and we were separated. But the sentence has hung in the air ever since.

Victor's farmhouse is not visible from the highway. To get to it we must go down a winding road, under trees, and then we come upon the house as a surprise, a two story house with a sagging front porch. It needs painting, and the guttering is rusted, but it's a big, pleasant house with a front porch and wide windows.

Victor brings the car to a stop under an ancient walnut tree and looks at the house a little balefully. "You think I'm crazy, don't you? I can tell what you're thinking."

"No, no, I don't. Really I like it."

"Do you?" he says, looking pleased. "It does have a very nice fireplace. Fieldstone. And there's this bedroom up under the eaves I'll bet you'll like . . ."

The inside of the house is musky and smells of mice; the stairs look unsafe. But Victor is right. I do like it and the moment I walk into the bedroom under the eaves I covet it. In an instant I've set it all up — a table to write on under the windows, a chair or two, maybe, and bookshelves. The perfect place. All my life I've done that — putting myself to sleep making the perfect study or hide-out for myself. Even when I was nine years old I had a hide-out in the back of Daddy's hardware store — a packing case house that contained all the necessities.

"It's perfect," I tell Victor as I look out the windows. "I've always wanted a room like this away from the house. In a place like this I wouldn't sit around writing shopping lists, I'll bet."

Victor leans against the doorway watching me prowl around. He's gratified, I know, that I like the place—I can sense the expansiveness coming over him.

"Well, why don't you use it for a hidy-hole?" he says, "I won't be moving in for awhile and anyway there're four bedrooms. So why not?"

I can't believe it, am suspicious of my luck. Why should Victor give me a bedroom? But a certain childish avarice in me is deeply pleased. Of course I deserve it—I deserve a room to myself and anything else I'm ever likely to be given. All that and more too. And anyway some twisted socialism which lies deeper than politics can ever go *gives* me the room. *Each according to his needs.* And I need that room.

I choose to ignore a certain cautiousness—peasant I suppose it is—that tells me that nothing is ever given free, whole and without thought of cost.

But all those jewels laid at Margarite's feet wouldn't have looked any better to me—not as good, come to that—as an empty room with south windows and a door I could close on the world.

"If you're *sure*," I tell Victor, "why, I'd love it. It's just in the mornings anyway and I'll try not to get in your way . . ."

"It's all yours, then. And I'll bring up a table from downstairs you can use to write on. I don't even bother to lock the place since there's nothing here now worth stealing, so just come in whenever you feel like it. There it is."

Even Faust put up a little more fight than I do. I fall in a moment, would have taken the room, anyway, even if I'd known the cost beforehand.

2

In the afternoon, under the flaming September leaves, my friend Diana and I jog through the woods along the trail we follow three times a week. Diana lives out possibilities for me that I am unable to follow myself. And I do the same thing for her. She has been married twice, neither time for long, and there is often a man with whom she shares her bed and wine for awhile but these connections never last long. She is a woman too used to having her own way, to following her own bent, and men get in her way. She's a sculptor and she sometimes whiles away entire nights hacking away at a recalcitrant piece of wood with an axe, shaping and hewing. I envy her her singlemindedness, the uncompromising quality of her life, and she envies me Isabel and Felicity, and sometimes she even envies me Walter's companionship and his willingness to bring me hot milk in the middle of the night.

On this particular afternoon, Diana is urging me to come with her the next day when she does her weekly stint at P-Wing doing occupational therapy with those people who have taken a leave—temporary or otherwise—from the dailiness the rest of us stumble on in.

"It'll only be a couple of hours," Diana says, not even breathing hard, "and you ought to get out of yourself more."

"I don't really want to," I say, spacing out my words carefully so they won't take too much wind. Diana's eight years older than I am but that, clearly, doesn't make any difference. She played on the basketball team—I gather she was a star center—when she was at Purdue, and she's kept in shape ever since. I haven't played games since I was ten and realized there wasn't a hope in hell I'd ever get to be a boy no matter how fast I could run or how high I could climb a tree. Diana was appalled the first time we went jogging together two years ago. After quarter of a mile I had a stitch in my side and was panting.

"You ought to be ashamed, letting your body go as flabby as that," she said, looking cross.

"Well, I'm not fat," I said, feeling wrongfully accused.

"So what? I suppose you care about your looks. But what good does it do you being thin if you can't run a quarter of a mile?"

Diana works at developing endurance as though she were in training for some Amazon army. She rides, swims, skiis; she plays tennis, squash, has taken up Kundalini yoga. And of course she jogs.

"I don't care if you want to come to P-Wing or not," Diana says. "You ought to develop your social conscience more."

"I don't know anything about working with clay."

"What's there to know? We just sit at this long table making pinch pots. Most people make ashtrays. Don't tell me you couldn't make an ashtray."

"Maybe," I say, knowing that is the quickest way to shut Diana up. She thinks *maybe* means yes, but I know it means no.

I feel guilty about my lack of social conscience but not enough to do anything about it.

We cross over the narrow iron footbridge, the place that marks my three miles, and I come gratefully to a halt, breathing heavily, while Diana charges on ahead. Unencumbered, she lengthens her stride, something she's always urging me to do. In comparison to my painful lumbering she's practically sprinting.

I move over to the edge of the path, walking gently up and down, keeping out of the way of other joggers panting past. My sweatsoaked shirt and flushed cheeks mark me as respectable. For all the others know, I may have already jogged twelve miles through these winding wooded trails.

Walter worries that I might have heart failure on one of these jogs, but my real worries are far less dramatic. Blistered feet, aching shins, the danger of tripping over a tree root and breaking out my front teeth — these are my fears. I'm just less brave than when I was ten. I think with pride of the time I took a dare and climbed to the top of the gymnasium — thirty feet, straight up.

The gymnasium was built of large, square stones and there was one spot where the entrance jutted out from the main wall where we could climb up the corner, something like a mountain climber going up a chimney. Several of the boys had accomplished this feat but I was the first girl to make it all the way to the top. My hands were sweaty and my knees weak but I hid my fear by strutting around and waving to the faces below. However, something has happened to me between the ages of ten and thirty to turn me into a coward. Once I admitted there was no way out of spending the rest of my life as a girl, I seemed to have become practically overnight, cowardly, living life once removed.

I envy Diana her ability to keep to what's important. When she's in her studio she doesn't answer the telephone or the doorbell; the rest of the world could fall away in an earthquake and she probably wouldn't notice. But of course she doesn't *have* to. Husband and children aren't going to pound on her door asking if there isn't some more toilet paper lying around somewhere or wanting to know if Patsy's been given his supper.

Yet all of this is beside the point. I didn't have to get married. I didn't have to have two children. Nobody held a gun to my head. I chose to do both these things, clearly. But why? What prevented me from making the kind of life Diana has if that's what I admire so much?

Diana once told me that when she was a little girl she was prim and proper. She took ballet lessons and put her dolls to bed every night. While I was playing baseball she was turning on point and fluffing up her tutu.

And I've noticed before that it's the gaps that bother us. The unfinished parts of ourselves. The problem with me is that nothing seems finished—there's nothing but gaps. There I am, running around from gap to gap, trying to stick a husband in this one and a handful of manuscripts in that, and then a baby in one and, oh lord, I see that whatever I stuff in them the gaps are widening, the gaps are gaping, and I'm going to be swept out into the void.

While I take a shower in Diana's apartment I can hear her through the wall putting on the kettle, sliding cups back onto shelves. Even in the small ways Diana has order in her life.

"How're things with you and Elliot?" I ask her when I come in the kitchen, running my fingers through my wet hair. Elliot's been with Diana for two months now, about as long as any of them last. He's a gynecologist whose wife left him, and I've never liked him much but Diana says that, in spite of his profession, he's a whiz in bed.

"Do you think," Diana says, sliding a cup of tea across the table to me, "that I'm an overbearing person?"

"Yes," I answer without hesitation. "But I like you anyway."

"Elliot says I'm overbearing, that I'm always telling him what to do, but I don't know. It seems to me I'm perfectly willing to let him lead his own life. I *want* him to. But he seems to think it's some kind of major crime when I forget to telephone him when I say I will. I don't remember *anything* like that when I'm working but he takes it as a personal affront. He thinks I do it on purpose in some weird way just to assert my power."

"You aren't too patient with other people's weaknesses."

"You know Mother raised us all to be tough as nails. And Dad never did anything except stir up glue fumes down in the basement from all those model ships he was always putting together — that and dropping his Jockey shorts with little smears of shit in them back behind the radiators. What use was that?"

This is old ground which we've pawed over listlessly a hundred times, like archaeologists sifting earth through a sieve. I know all about Diana's mother — a Legal Aid lawyer who spends most of her time down at the county jail.

"If I didn't always feel so *bad* every time I get fed up with a man. Mother all over again. The way she sort of eased Dad out of the household. Well, no, she didn't, either. That's not fair. He eased himself out, packing his suitcase one Sunday afternoon and riding the bus over to his sister's. A visit that lasted for about ten years though he used to come over every week or two and eat supper and putter around in the basement for awhile. It was kind of pitiful, when I think about it, the way he used to slip out of the house about ten o'clock, letting himself out the side door, to catch the bus back to Aunt Beth's. Oh, why is family life so awful?

18

Mother did sort of swallow him up the way spiders — is it? — do away with their mates after they've screwed, or whatever it is spiders do."

Diana looks moodily into her tea cup and I know all the signs. Her remorse always leads her straight to her neat row of cookbooks on the shelf and she'll spend the afternoon cooking an elaborate meal that will fill Elliot with expansive joy. But afterwards, when the leftovers are put away in the refrigerator with Saran Wrap over their tops, Diana will pick a fight with Elliot about some trifle — the toothpaste he forgot to buy or the newspaper he left strewn over the coffee table.

"And there you are with Walter," Diana says, including me, too, in her anger. "Like two little peas in a pod, or like three year olds warming your cold feet on each other's tummies and tucking the sheets around each other's chins."

"I can't help it if I have a good marriage," I tell Diana, holding no grudge. "There has to be one around, doesn't there, as a prototype or something?"

Walter comes home, as usual, at 5:45 on the dot. I hear him hanging his jacket in the closet and putting his briefcase on the hall table. "I'm back!" he cries joyfully. For Walter, just getting safely inside his own house every evening is a miracle, an occasion for rejoicing. The day with its dangers has been safely navigated and Walter has brought his little craft back to safety once more. The girls run into the hallway squealing. I find it odd that they are both Daddy's girls since I was the other kind of girl myself. A Momma's girl. And I'm a little suspicious of Daddy's girls. I'm afraid they'll end up just sitting around having babies and making crocks of pickles for some man who reminds them of Daddy.

Walter comes into the kitchen with a daughter in each arm, looking dazed with pleasure. The kitchen is a wreck as it always is when I cook, but Walter looks at the carnage as though even that gives him pleasure. Which, in fact, it does. He's another who loves making order out of chaos in quiet little ways.

He puts the girls down at the kitchen table where, before he arrived, they were squabbling over puzzles. Now they immediately scamper away to another part of the house, Walter's presence the catalyst that makes them suddenly bold and cheerful.

"What happened to you today?" Walter asks as he always does. Walter and I enjoy the mundane trivialities of each other's days. Walter tells me what he had for lunch in the Union; I tell him about seeing a mouse scamper across the kitchen floor. We always marvel that we have survived these hours apart from one another. But today I say, "Oh, nothing much happened. Diana and I went jogging, as usual."

There must have been a reason, even then, that early on, why I did not say, "Oh, and another thing, too. Victor's bought himself a farmhouse out in the country and he's letting me use one of the rooms for a writing place." But no. My lips close on that little piece of information like a cat clamping its teeth on a mouse's backbone. That, that one little thing, I will have as a secret. A small thing, a trifle after all.

But Walter seems not to notice anything sly about me. His thoughts are elsewhere. I know, because I've lived with Walter for five years and we often pick up each other's thoughts, that he is now thinking about Fassbinder and his session today with him. Fassbinder — what he says and what Walter says back — occupies Walter's thoughts a good deal these days and he tries, gamefully, to let me in on these convoluted discussions. It's not Walter's fault that my mind wanders. It's exactly the same as when somebody starts telling, in detail, a dream he had the night before. I immediately blank out and start yawning. I don't know how Fassbinder stays awake through all those dreams he has to listen to.

Walter started going to Fassbinder three years ago, not long after his father died — after Leon gave himself that stroke yelling at a mechanic in a Mercedes garage. It was a boiling day in Boston — 90° even before nine o'clock — and Walter's father had just gotten the Mercedes back after eight hours in the garage for the air conditioner to be fixed. That morning he climbed in the car, turned on the air conditioner, and it emptied a cupful of water on his feet. The roar of indignant rage he directed at the mechanic guilty of this perfidy burst a blood vessel in his head and he keeled over dead.

Walter sort of went to pieces at his father's death.

Not that he had been close to his father. On the contrary. He couldn't stand him alive, but he was bothered by his being dead. Uneasiness descended on him. Disaster, he realized, was always impending, lurking everywhere. Frantically he took measures — checking on the furnace three times a night, sniffing out mysterious burning smells which nobody else could detect. And it wasn't unreasonable of Walter to elicit Fassbinder's help in tracking down this sense of doom to its source, like searching out the dragon in his lair. I even encouraged Walter to telephone Dr. Fassbinder, and held his hand while he made that first, terrifying appointment.

But I don't know. I've lost patience with the whole thing or something. I don't care anymore if Fassbinder chuckles at something Walter says nor does it seem very earthshaking to me that Fassbinder announces one day that Walter's fascination with paintings, his love of colors and shapes on canvas, arise from some anal fixation.

The real point is, why should Fassbinder be let in on all the little stories that Walter and I have always shared together? That was the thing, from the very beginning, that has set us apart from other couples we know: we have shared everything.

The very first time we met, at a party in Madison where we were both graduate students, I spotted Walter almost as soon as I came into the room. I was always on the lookout for other people standing around at the edges of other people's conversations and Walter had spotted me, too. We came together in the middle of the room by the crackers and cheese. I thought at first that Walter was a Southerner because in his progress across the room, he said excuse me very time he had to pass near someone else. And when he came closer his round face and gentle expression also looked as though it could have come from Georgia or Mississippi, though I didn't realize until later that he reminded me, in some obscure way, of my brother Olson. A certain guilelessness. I was only momentarily discouraged to hear Boston in his voice since it transpired that I hadn't been far wrong after all. Nina was from Tidewater, Virginia.

21

Still, on the surface at least, our worlds were very different — Walter's Boston and Harvard and mine Kellam, Arkansas, and the University of North Carolina. The surprising thing was that under that surface we were amazingly alike.

That first evening we went through a catechism out of both our childhoods: favorite color? Blue. What do you think about when you're trying to go to sleep at night? Lying on fat cushions in a pink tent. Earliest memory? Of course we couldn't have exactly the same earliest memory but they were similar. Mine of the room in which I was born, seeing yellow lights sway over my head. Walter's first memory was of lying on his back in the grass and seeing what may have been the sun dance in the sky. It was almost a relief when one of us said "Food?" and Walter said, "Bay scallops broiled in a little butter," and I said "Turnip greens and corn bread."

When we married, a year from the time we first met, we knew that our marriage was a wonder, a closeness to be cherished. Even at parties we often sneaked off to a corner to talk, a little guiltily, to each other.

So why should we let Fassbinder in our little closed shop? Threesomes are always troublesome.

"It wasn't a very good session today," Walter says while I cut the cores out of apples before stuffing them with nuts and honey. "I got off on the wrong foot, somehow. As soon as I came in I saw he'd moved two bookcases. I tried to figure out why although I hate those guessing games. Twenty questions. I say, 'Why did you switch your bookcases around?' and he says, 'Why do you think? What comes to mind?' He'll never tell me the answer anyway, even if I guess right. He just goes on to the next question. 'Why does it disturb you that I moved my bookcases?' And then we start all over again. Finally I got down to the interesting part."

As soon as Walter says "interesting part" I click out. I know in advance, now, the way the thing is going to go. I know that Walter is disturbed by seeing objects moved into unexpected places and forming new, frightening patterns. If objects can be *moved* they can be *removed*, etc. etc. I know that we're heading for the lilac bush again under which Walter saw the little neighbor

22

girl with her pants down and had the terrible revelation: *Girls don't have one!*.   But if this is the terrible thing Walter has to worry about — that what can be moved can also be removed — then in my opinion he might as well forget about it. Who does he think is going to sneak up now and cut it off when he isn't looking? But there I go, making snide remarks about Fassbinder's interpretations.

I keep my mouth shut on that as I keep it shut on my windfall of the day.

After supper, while Walter is reading *Little Fur Family* to the girls once again, a daughter snuggled into each arm, I go ahead to take my bath although I know that this is going to disappoint Walter when he finds out. What he likes is to sit on the closed toilet seat, talking while I bathe, scrubbing my back, handing me a dry towel when I come out. Those little intimacies matter so much to him. When he was growing up, an only child, fat and lonely, he made up an imaginary younger sister to share everything with. And now, of course, he has me.

No longer fat, Walter isn't what you could call skinny, either. He's tall and what we call in Arkansas big-boned. The kind of hands and feet he still needs to grow into like some great, gawky puppy. He'll always look younger than he is because his face is broad and unlined, and his fair eyebrows give him an astonished look.

I lock the door of the bathroom practically on Patsy's tail. He lies down heavily on my dressing gown which I've dropped on the floor and starts chewing delicately at one of the buttons though I wish I had the heart to put him out. If I do, though, he'll only sit at the door and make wet snuffling noises at the crack and I already feel a little guilty about shutting Walter out without having Patsy on my conscience too. So I put up with his sorrowful eyes and the gentle nipping with which he chews the button.

I crouch by the bathtub, watching the water run, pondering a question I ponder fairly frequently under these circumstances. When I was a freshman in college I took a personality test — we all had to take it shut up in the gymnasium one hot September afternoon — and among other questions there was this one:

I would rather take a bath than a shower.

(a) yes

(b) no

(c) no preference

I debated for some time the correct answer to this question. (I was certain there *were* right answers in spite of the man in charge saying there weren't). If you preferred taking a bath did it mean that you had a tendency to hide from harsh reality by escaping into the warm wetness of the womb, or did it mean that you were sensuous and could accept pleasure? I still don't know what the right answer is. I chose (c) as I did on that test everytime I was in doubt. No preference. No opinion. My score on that test must have rated me a zombie.

Usually I get into the tub and crouch there on my heels, washing myself rapidly and efficiently with a washrag, but tonight I linger, sitting in the water with my legs outstretched. I even look down at myself and consider my body.

I've always been skinny, rounding out briefly when I was pregnant but flattening down again quickly afterwards. No flab yet. I have toughened up since I've been jogging with Diana and I've always been glad to be thin, never doubting that Walter would like me however I was — fat, thin, short and squat — whatever. We would never, we assured each other that first evening we met, put any stock in such things as the flesh. That was on a minor level of importance altogether. And, since I married Walter, I have not wasted my time wondering how other men see me. But, say, just say for a moment, that some man other than Walter was watching me sitting there in the bathtub — would another man — take Victor for instance — find me attractive?

(a) yes

(b) no

(c) no opinion

I'm pretty sure that Victor would answer (b). Don't my hipbones stick out too much and aren't my knees too knobby? I'm sure of it. But still, still, my breasts, though small, are as plump as plums. And that long torso and flat belly *does* have a certain elegance. My hips aren't too wide and my thighs don't let a whole

24

wedge of light shine between them—press together as I would—as they did when I was fifteen. So maybe it's not so bad after all. But who except Walter is going to see?

He's just turning off the girls' light when I come in to kiss them goodnight.

"You've already taken your bath," he says, disappointed, a little reproachfully. One of the little pleasures he's been looking forward to gone down the drain.

"I'm just tired, Walter."

"Oh, you should go to bed early, then," he says quickly in case I may think he's selfish and only thinking about his own pleasure.

The girls look very sweet tucked in their beds. When I'm leaning over Isabel's bed, my neck caught in the vise of her plump arms, she whispers in my ear, "Could we got to town tomorrow and you buy us some shoes?"

"No promises," I say warily, having learned from bitter experience the danger in promising anything. "Maybe."

"Will you?"

"I will if I can. No promises."

"Everybody else has shoes," Isabel says reproachfully. "And you forgot to send us mats for rest time again. We have to use fuzzy rugs that belong to Mrs. Faraday."

"All right, Isabel, I'll see what I can do," I tell her, disentangling myself from her grip. It's too bad that a child who likes to be correct in every detail, as Isabel does, has to be stuck with a mother who is incapable of being correct, but that's one of life's little jokes. Maybe Isabel will grow up being more flexible and tolerant because of having me for a mother but I doubt it. She'll probably grow up to join a country club, the Episcopal Church, and the Junior League.

Since I've married Walter I've fallen in with many of his habits. I don't intend to. It just happens. I never used to go to bed at 7:30 at night but now I do regularly, to read, my head propped by three pillows, or to watch television over the tops of my toes. It seems perfectly natural now to retreat to the bedroom as soon as the girls are in bed, to close the shutters and shut the door. This is

Walter's best time of day. He loves it when he can climb into bed with me, all warm from his shower, the harsh world and its battles banished outside our white shutters. The girls are safe in their beds, and we are lying side by side with Patsy snuffling and thumping under the bed, hunting imaginary fleas through his fur.

Walter stretches out in pleasure between the sheets, sighs, and picks up the book he's left, with bookmark neatly in place, on his bedside table.

But his pleasure is too great.

Almost as soon as he settles down he remembers that there are dangerous forces all around that would like to take this little haven from him. Soon he puts his book down, puts on his dressing gown, and slippers, and begins the first of the nocturnal prowls through the house, checking on locked doors and windows, on the possibility that the taint in the air, that smell he can't identify, might be smoke starting to seep from crossed wires behind the stove, from faulty insulation in the dryer, from a tube deep inside the television set in the kitchen.

"Why can't you just trust to luck?" I say, when he finally returns. "I mean there's no end to the possibilities. Maybe all that old plaster up there will fall on us in the night. Or a meteor will crash through the roof and squash us."

"But those aren't likely to happen," Walter says patiently. "You read all the time, though, about people being trapped when their house burns down or being murdered by some burglar."

"If you surprise a burglar at his work he's going to be a lot more apt to kill you," I say reasonably. "If a burglar came right in this bedroom and took the television set I'd pretend to be asleep. I sure wouldn't go padding around the house looking for him."

"But what I want to do, you see, is to stop the burglar when he's still just fiddling with the window catch."

"You can't think of everything, Walter," I tell him, but I know I'm wasting my breath. If Fassbinder hasn't been able to do anything in three years, what makes me think that by stating the obvious I'll be able to put Walter's fears to rest? "Maybe the danger's not something as obvious as a fire, anyway," I say reasonably. "Maybe what worries you is old age or something like that."

"Old age doesn't bother me at all. If I can just get us all through the years safely until then I'll consider myself lucky."

Which, oddly enough, is true. I can easily imagine Walter sitting in the sun in his nineties, smiling his sweet smile, having only one last thing to worry about—keeping me going until he manages to die before me.

We settle down under our lamps, tipping our books to the light, the only sound that of plaintive crickets in the grass outside the windows.

But not for long. Walter puts his book down, clicks off his light, slides over to my side of the bed, and burrows his knees into mine.

"You could turn off the light, you know," he says.

It's not out of prudishness that Walter won't make love with the light on but because he doesn't want to disturb the evil forces that lie in wait all around the house, just waiting until our attention is turned elsewhere before they spring, rattling the locks and pushing at the windows. They shouldn't see us enjoying ourselves.

Not that our lovemaking is all that ecstatic. Since Fassbinder, a certain self-consciousness has crept in. Maybe some people like that—the third presence watching over the shoulder adding some extra fillip. But when I make love with Walter knowing that on the next day he may well report to Fassbinder the whole thing, step by step, detail by detail, I think oh, what the hell. The mere thought tires me out.

I can just hear the whole scene in Fassbinder's office—a voice, Walter's presumably, saying, "Well, then, after we kissed I started moving my hands down . . . oh slowly, yes, uh huh, pretty slowly . . . right, right, to her buttocks and then I started tipping her back since by that time I was ready . . ."

It's like a recipe over the radio. And what's more I imagine I can hear, like another station cutting in, Fassbinder's *basso profundo* making suggestions. He's right in here, under the covers with us, watching with a look of mild boredom on his face.

So I fall into formula and it all comes to its usual conclusion pretty fast. Nevertheless, when we finished, Walter hastens to assure me that it was beautiful. He scoops me up in his arms to kiss me, proving he's not one of those lovers who finish sex and instantly starts snoring like a pig.

"Was that all right for you?" Walter asks anxiously, as he always does.

"Of course," I tell him, kissing him on the ear so he won't worry.

Walter smiles back, his gentle smile, and slides easily into his first sleep of the night. He will be up, later, padding around like a bear stirring from hiberation, but for now he supposes that I will keep us safe.

I'm restless and vaguely hungry. I consider going to the kitchen and making myself a peanut butter sandwich, but peanut butter isn't exactly what I want. I lie awake wondering if other women feel this way after lovemaking and figure that many do. Not Olivia though, I'll bet, curled up on her warm Roman sheets. I'm pretty sure that Olivia slides immediately into a wonderful sleep after she makes love with her curly headed satyr.

3

The next morning, after I take Isabel and Felicity to nursery school, I hurry back home and, like a thief, I carry books, typewriter, and paper from my study under the eaves and put it in the car. I'm filled with glee as I back out the driveway — I feel sure that once in my room — once in my secret room — that the realities, the nuisances of my life will fall away and I will be set free to descend, like Alice falling into the rabbit hole, straight back into childhood, even infancy. That I will find the central thread, the one that can be followed back to the beginning and out again.

Again I will write my first sentence: *Beginning at the beginning with the bright light in that oily little room in the Kellam Hospital where, hanging upside down like a pear on a limb, I blinked my eyes at the dim shapes swimming in and out of my vision* . . . and I will follow the thread along its inevitable unraveling.

Yet, when I let myself a little timidly in Victor's backdoor, alone with the smell of mice and the dripping faucet making a brown ring in the kitchen sink, I don't feel as pleased as I expected, somehow. I seem to have hurried all this way, expecting to meet someone who didn't show up.

Nevertheless, I labor up the stairs with all the things I need to make a study and find that, true to his word, Victor has brought a wooden table and chair from downstairs and set them up in front of the windows. So really I have everything I need. I could be in the North Woods as far as Walter and the girls are concerned, and the only creatures around — and they certainly don't care about me or about the pecking noises of my typewriter — are the squirrels running across the roof and two bluejays scolding from the walnut trees.

I sit in my chair and put sentences on paper and by 12:30 when I must leave to pick up the girls, I have forgotten my disappointment when I came into the house and knew that it was empty.

But by afternoon, there is nothing but dailiness.

At three o'clock, instead of being with Diana in P-Wing making pinchpots with paranoids and neurotics, I'm in the Kiddie World shop for children, back in the shoe section.

When the salesman, a worn little man with hair growing out of his nose asks, "What can I do for you young ladies today?" Isabel makes him guess the shoe she wants. He points until he comes to the right one—a red shoe with a fringe down to the toes. The salesman raises his eyebrows when he picks it up, looking in my direction, but I smile brightly. I don't care what the girls wear on their feet as long as we can get this expedition over quickly.

"That shoe runs a little wide," the salesman says doubtfully. "The same kind for you, little lady?" he asks Felicity.

"Do we get balloons?"

"Something better. For pretty little girls like you I'll bet I could find lollypops."

"Purple?"

"For you I will try to find purple," the salesman says, winking.

"People're always giving us lollypops," Isabel says.

"Don't be such a spoiled brat," I tell her when the salesman goes off to look for the shoes but she just shrugs her shoulders and gets a stubborn look on her face.

I hate the strain of taking the girls shopping and I hate these long waits that we seem doomed to suffer in each other's company. We seem to wait endlessly in dentists' offices, pediatricians' offices, in the check-out line at supermarkets. And try as I will, I'm no good at making conversation with two and three-year-olds. I'm no good as a mother in these ways; I hate having my train of thought broken and I hate having to be always on the alert.

"Look at that little boy over there getting sneakers," I say now.

They go right on shrieking and trying to pull each other's socks off. And why should they look at the little boy, for heaven's sake? There's nothing the least bit interesting about him.

"How many nursery rhymes do you know?" I say, trying another tack. "Come on, let's see. Who knows the most? How about 'Rubba dub dub, three men in a tub.' Do you know that one?"

"Allsey owlsey woo woo," Felicity shrieks and slides out of her chair, something I've been dreading all along. "Wo, woo," she says, flapping her arms and running up and down with Isabel at her heels. Isabel knows that by following Felicity she can get by with more than she otherwise could since Felicity is clearly too little to have any sense.

"Come back, girls," I say weakly, knowing that I'm being one of those mothers that other people glare at. The kind who sit and pretend not to see what their children are up to. I have no control. Most other mothers don't, either, I'm convinced, but they are cleverer at hiding their weaknesses than I am. They whisper in their children's ears, "If you want a chocolate soda after this you are going to sit down *now*."

I just sit with a silly, glassy smile on my face, watching Felicity and Isabel charge up and down as though it has nothing to do with me.

They come back only when the salesman emerges from the storeroom with his arms full of boxes.

But it's bad news. I see that as soon as he sits down in the low stool that puts him at an immediate disadvantage. "Those shoes your daughter wants run a little wide," he says. "I have them in the little girl's size but not in the other one's. She's got narrow feet. Only thing I've got that'll fit her is these."

He takes a perfectly plain brown oxford out of a box, the same kind of oxford I wore all through my childhood. Buster Browns. I always liked them myself but Isabel frowns and starts shaking her head.

When the salesman tries to take her foot to put the shoe on she kicks up and down and grabs the arms of the chair preparatory to shutting her eyes and making that awful keening noise.

"Try the other child," I say quickly, and the salesman does, in relief. The red shoe with the fringe slips as easily as though it's greased onto Felicity's plump foot. She holds still for him to put

31

the second one on and then she slides to the floor and walks up and down, as decorously as an old woman going to church. Her fat smile makes Isabel frown even more darkly.

There's going to be hell to pay. I know that beyond a shadow of a doubt and so does the salesman who keeps pulling at the lose skin above his Adam's apple.

"The brown ones are the only ones they have that fit you," I tell Isabel, trying to sound firm. Isabel shakes her head and sticks out her lower lip. "Then you'll just have to go on wearing the ones you have."

Isabel doesn't appear to have heard. She remains sitting rigidly in the chair with her feet and lower lip thrust out.

While I pay for Felicity's shoes she walks in circles in front of the chair which Isabel appears determined to occupy for the next twenty years. Felicity is braver, or more stupid, than I thought she was. Isabel, by the looks of her, might spring at any moment and devour Felicity without leaving even the palms of her hands and the soles of her feet.

"Well, what shall we do about your other little girl?" the salesman says as he hands Felicity her sandals in a box along with a grape lollypop.

"Any ideas?"

The salesman looks a little taken aback by this question but at least he takes action. He takes a red lollypop from the box under the counter and approaches Isabel with it, holding it between thumb and forefinger the way people who are nervous hold out bones to dogs.

Isabel never moves; she just sits there with her eyes bulging, her hands stiff on the arms of the chair.

"Put her sandals in a box. I'll have to carry her out."

A rear attack may have surprise value so I put my hands under Isabel's arms and yank from behind. She hangs onto the chair arms but I'm stronger than she is and she finally has to let go.

She wails, a terrible, eery noise. She is heartbroken, murderous. I walk through the store like one walking through leech infested water, looking neither right nor left, Felicity hanging onto the bottom of my jacket.

We go past shoes, pajamas, underwear, the door is in sight,

32

when Isabel's breath catches halfway down its descent, she makes a fluttery gasp, and points. "I want that," she says in a small, drowned voice.

I am so astonished by the silence that I halt right where I am.

"That dress right there," Isabel says.

The dress she's pointing to is white with drawn work across the chest. I know at a glance that it's expensive but I ease my way over to it anyway, clutching Isabel, purse, bundle of shoes, and find the price tucked inside a sleeve.

"Twenty-five dollars, Isabel. Too much."

"I want it," she says, tears filling her eyes again and balancing there.

She has me in a bad spot and she knows it. I've already deprived her, somehow, of the shoes she wanted and have given them to Felicity. I surely owe her something for that outrage.

"You don't have anywhere to wear a dress like that," I tell her, being reasonable. Children don't dress to the teeth anymore even for birthday parties as they did when I was a child.

"I would wear it for Daddy," Isabel says in a small voice, sucking in her lower lip.

"Oh lord! Daddy likes you in anything, Isabel. You don't have to wear a twenty-five dollar dress for Daddy."

Everytime Isabel says something like that I know that, some-how, I've been a terrible mother and I feel pained but helpless as though Isabel has some infection that penicillin won't curb. That terrible, submissive desire to please, as destructive as any germ.

Isabel's lips start quivering. Tears roll down her cheeks. Probably she's going to hold it against me the rest of her life—I'm the witch-like mother who wouldn't buy her what she needed to confirm her femininity. And the fact that I won't bind her feet, either, nor knock out one of her front teeth when she begins menstruating doesn't mean that she won't manage to bind herself as thoroughly as though she were in a strait jacket. And whatever happens I will get the blame, almost certainly. I can just see her, thirty years from now, telling the story of this terrible afternoon to an updated version of Dr. Fassbinder and making his couch all slick with her tears.

But I'm very near to throwing in the sponge—I will buy

Isabel shoes she'll have to slide around inside, buy her a twenty-five dollar dress to dance in front of Daddy in. Anything for a little peace.

However, misjudging my silence, she starts yelling again, roaring with her face turning red, and my sympathy for her goes. I don't care if she has to walk around in the snow barefooted. I don't care if she has to sell matches. All I want is to get rid of her.

I make it to the car, slide Isabel into the backseat, put Felicity in the front, and start driving. Hand and foot take over and I realize only when I've turned into the quiet, leafy campus, where I'm heading.

In the parking lot beside Atkinson Hall I get Isabel, still in stocking feet and still yelling, from the back seat, Felicity from the front, and start toiling up the stairs. I've developed strong arm muscles from carrying the two of them around but even so I have to lean against the wall with my shoulder and push my way up. I'm panting and staggering by the time I get to the third floor.

Walter's door is open, luckily, and I'm able to go straight in. He looks up in alarm from his desk and the student who is with him actually draws his knees up against his chest as though he thinks I'm going to shoot him in the stomach.

But as soon as I put Isabel on the rug in front of Walter's desk, she stops yelling. In fact, there is a sudden silence in which Walter clears his throat.

"If your daughter is going to have shoes on her feet you will have to get them," I say, and walk out the door I have just come in.

Behind me, silence. After all, it's a great treat to be allowed to go to Daddy's office and the girls aren't going to spoil a lucky break like that by misbehaving. Walter will manage very well; the power of novelty is all in his favor.

When I get in the car, I head up the hill toward University Hospital to get in on Diana's last hour in the psycho ward; maybe I want to expiate my sins.

And certainly my mother would approve since DOING SOMETHING FOR OTHERS could have been her motto. If there wasn't a single thing you had to give to another person, my mother was fond of saying, you could at least give him a smile and brighten up his day.

So as I go in the big doors of University Hospital I plaster a big smile on my face.

I know my way around the medical sections fairly well since that was where I had Isabel and Felicity and I go there occasionally to visit people who've had babies or operations. But I've never been inside P-Wing. It's not that I haven't known people checked into P-Wing but I have avoided visiting them. I rationalize and say that if I were there I wouldn't want people from the outside coming in and bothering me. The truth is, though, that I feel P-Wing is sinister. People are probably locked in padded cells or laced up in strait jackets and stacked up like so many cords of wood. This is what happens to people who don't do what they're supposed to.

I tiptoe down the corridor—disturbing nothing, seeing nobody—until I come to a door with Craft Room written on it in Gothic lettering. All the heads lift from the pats of grey clay and stare at me. I smile, making them a free gift of it, but nobody smiles back. They don't like me, I can tell. Their eyes go through my smile like acid through copper plate and my smile withers instantly and dies.

Diana, sitting on the far side of the table, tries to smooth over my entrance.

"This is my friend, Lee, everybody. The one I told you about."

I feel it would be cowardly to walk all the way around the table to sit in a safe spot beside her and I'm too flustered to choose my spot with care. I walk straight ahead and squeeze onto the bench between a thin, wispy girl and a thin, hairy boy. They don't seem overjoyed to have me there between them and give me hardly any room, but I'm good at fitting myself into tight spaces. I keep my elbows in and don't breath much.

Diana rolls a ball of clay across the table to me, and I pick it up and weigh it in my hand.

"What am I supposed to do with this?" I say, trying for the lightly facetious note.

35

"Stuff it up your ass," the hairy boy says under his breath. Nobody else appears to have heard this remark and I decide that I might have imagined it.

The hairy boy is making what I first take to be an ashtray but when I look more closely I see that it's a sloppily made crown of thorns. I think of comments I could make but decide against making them.

The wispy girl on my left is making the head of a wispy, wistful looking girl much like herself.

"Nice head," I say to her.

She gives me a long, sad look. "I think it stinks," she says.

I squeeze on my ball of clay but it is surprisingly hard and I don't have much space to work in. With some difficulty I manage to break off a small piece of clay from the big lump and begin rolling it back and forth between my fingers and the table. I remember doing this in grade school. It's the only thing I can think of to do with clay.

"She's going to make a snake," the boy on my right says, pointing to my effort. "Ha ha."

I give him a quick look but no, I've never seen his particular thin, rat-like face before.

"Or maybe she's going to make herself a nice little penis." He seems to think that's very funny.

To my surprise, the wispy girl comes to my defense. "You are such a jerk, Jeffrey," she says, leaning across me to hiss in his face. "You are the biggest first-class jerk in this whole building." She whispers in my ear, "You don't have to stay in here and listen to creeps, you know. Want to come down to my room for awhile?"

"Is that o.k.? You can leave here whenever you want to?"

"It's a free country," she says, shrugging her shoulders.

So I follow her, with relief, to the doorway.

"I just hate that Jeffrey," the girl says when we reach the hall. "His eyebrows are the exact same shape as my father's."

She looks a lot less wispy out here, more determined. In fact, she walks too fast so I have to hurry to keep up with her, and I see that she's one of those thin, ethereal looking people whose frail looks are deceptive.

"Do you know who my father is?" she says, giving me a sharp look. I shake my head.

"Bill Hooper, that's who."

"W. M. Hooper? The poet?"

"Yeah. I'm Chloe Hooper. *Chloe* for god's sake. He was responsible for that, too, the old fart. He set out from the very first day to ruin my life and oh boy, did he succeed."

Sitting against the wall of the hallway, so that we have to make a jog around her, there is a girl masturbating and sucking her thumb at the same time with an eery, manic look in her eyes. I look away fast and pretend that the sight is nothing to me — that I see things like that all the time.

"Oh for heaven's sake," Chloe says, stopping and looking down at the girl in disgust. "Hey, Lynette, you could go to your room to do that you know."

Lynette doesn't even look in our direction.

"You'd think they could at least keep her out of public display, wouldn't you?"

"What's wrong with her?"

"Oh, crazy. What else? But I mean she's really crazy. Not so much her father, with her, as it was her brother, or so the tale goes. Been having sex with her brother from the time she was five."

"Really?" I say, looking back over my shoulder. "Is that why she is the way she is?"

Chloe shrugs her shoulders and stands aside at the doorway of her room so I can go inside. "Who knows?"

Chloe sits crosslegged on the bed and I sit on the edge. She stares at me for some time, thoughtfully, coming or so I suppose, to some conclusion. "Well," she says finally, "which one was it with you? Mother or father?"

"Mother," I say instantly.

"Thought so," she says with satisfaction, leaning back against the headboard. "Nearly always tell. I get this gut feeling about mother people. Father people turn me off just like that." And she slices her hand through the air like a knife.

"What was so terrible about your father?"

Chloe's lips curl back over her teeth. "Oh my dear old Daddy.

37

I'll bet anything you know what he looks like — dust jackets and such — white fluffy hair like Jehovah Himself, and those blue eyes. Boy, I'll bet you thought he was fine looking, didn't you? Kindly and earthy and all that crap."

"Well . . ." I say uncertainly. Actually I did think he was both those things the one time I heard him give a reading of his own poetry. He won me over by the way he said "nekkid" instead of "naked" and by the way his boots were worn down at the heels as though he had spent time walking behind a mule.

"Don't believe all you see. Because that old man did a right job on me. Do you know that before I was three he used to feel me up? My mother was his third wife and young enough to be his granddaughter, practically, and even that wasn't young enough for him. Oh, the sweet bosom of the family. All those daddies and mommies and sisters and brothers. What a can of worms! What a mess! By the time we crawl out the other side we're old and haggard."

"But I don't see how . . ."

"Listen, just don't give me that crap, will you? Sure you see. You know what I'm talking about. Just too yellow to say so."

I can see it now, flicking in the back of Chloe's eyes — the light that informs prophets and crazies.

"As soon as we're born we've already got this mother and father. There they are. So just what am I supposed to do about it?"

"Free yourself," Chloe says, leaning forward and fixing me with those strange eyes of hers.

"Yeah, well, o.k., I'll see what I can do," I say uneasily, getting up from the bed and edging for the door.

"It's your goose going to get cooked. Just keep that in mind. I've done my duty so you better not go around blaming *me*. Your funeral."

"Well, thanks a lot for telling me," I say as I reach the door open it.

"You better believe it," Chloe says behind me in a bitter voice.

When I get home there are Isabel, Felicity and Walter in the kitchen. Walter is wearing old clothes and is covered with a fine dusting of flour. The girls are standing in chairs enthusiastically punching rabbits and cats out of cookie dough. A domestic scene to ease anybody's heart.

Isabel is wearing, as I knew she would be, a pair of shoes like Felicity's and although I could stick two fingers between the back of the shoe and her heel I think what the hell. If she gets blisters all over her feet she might learn a thing or two.

Walter gives me an apologetic smile over his shoulder.

"I know they're too big," he says, "but she wanted them so much . . ."

"And the dress too?" I ask suspiciously.

"No. No dress." He gives me a look that I think is meant to be meaningful. Probably he's asked the store to keep the dress until Christmas. By that time, I know very well, Isabel will have set her heart on something else. But I don't say anything.

Walter shoos the girls away from the oven and slides in a sheet of cookies. "Now we'll have to wait," he tells them, and they dance out of the kitchen to wait somewhere else. The cleaning up doesn't interest them.

"Don't you think it's bad to spoil the girls, so, Walter?" I ask him as we do the dishes. "They're too crazy about you anyway without your adding fuel to the flame."

He looks crestfallen and, yes, a little guilty.

"They're small such a short time. And Isabel looks so sweet in the shoes . . ."

"Oh, let her go around the rest of her life looking for some man as adoring as Daddy. What can I do about it? It's all a can of worms, anyway. What do I know about raising daughters? Maybe I ought to have had sons . . ."

"That's nonsense! You're a very good mother, Lee. Maybe I oughtn't to say it, but I think we're exceptional. We're so happy . . ."

"I know, I know," I say, but my spirits do not rise.

When the girls come in, checking on the cookies, Walter picks them up and hugs them against his ribs as though, by his love, he will crush any remaining bit of uncertainty my words might have left in his mind. He dances them up and down in a jaunty little two step and tells me to join in too.

So I put my hand on his shoulder and we dance across the kitchen that way, like some immensely heavy and clumsy animal, a dinosaur making its doomed way through the ferns.

4

On Saturday night there is a party at Victor's house. Since he will be moving, before long, into the farmhouse, I expect that he wants to get rid of his social obligations all at once while he's still in town. Walter thinks we should get to his house early so we can help Victor with things like setting out ashtrays and bowls of nuts — after all, Victor's a man living alone now — but I balk at this. I'm not enthusiastic about going to the party at all, much less early before the time when I can bury myself in the crowd.

And I'm having a worse case than usual of pre-party jitters.

"What should I wear?" I ask Walter as I always do though *he* doesn't know anything about it. All he ever says is that anything will be all right.

The problem is, do I want to be noticed or do I want to be able to merge into a corner somewhere behind the drinks table?

I flip through my clothes once again.

Most daring. A pale green chiffon dress — simple line from shoulder to floor which softens my angularity just enough. In a confident moment I could look elegant in that dress, maybe. Even mysteriously sexy. But if I hunch my shoulders and slouch I'll look like a teenager wearing one of her mother's dresses. I bought the green chiffon on sale in a confident moment and haven't had the courage to wear it yet. I look at it longingly tonight but haven't got the guts now, either.

Least daring. Tweed skirt and jacket. Good quality but dowdy. The kind of thing Englishwomen wear to tramp over the moors in.

In between. Blue and green skirt and a white silk blouse. Safe, but not exciting, though it's all I feel like coping with tonight. I always feel a little regretful when I choose safety but, after all, I will never make my mark in this world as a beauty.

By the time I've made up my mind what to wear there is no question any longer of arriving early to give Victor a hand with last minute details. The party is already in full swing when we come up the walk.

I have, as usual, my time of panic, coming into a room full of people all brightly and, seemingly, happily talking to each other. I'm certain at these moments that no one will speak to me all evening, that I will be shunted aside as I walk forlornly from group to group which all remain shut against me. I will have to spend the evening counting the prisms in the chandelier.

And though I know that worry about this possibility makes my eyes glaze (and who wants to talk to some woman with glazed eyes?) I am unable to help myself. Two minutes after I come into the room I'm still standing in the same spot, making a tiny half circle one way and then the other, doomed — I know it — to spend my evening in horrible isolation.

I despise this in myself and wonder, as I make my little half turns, smiling my glazed smile, where I can have gotten the notion that to be a *woman* necessarily entails enticement, seduction? But I know very well where — from my mother first of all. A lesson I pointedly ignored at the time but which I must not have been totally immune to since I remember only too well the indignity I felt, rattling around in a nearby empty college dormitory on Saturday nights, moving like a wraith through rooms occupied by girls big as blimps, the only noise being the gentle hissing of wheelchairs moving in flotillas down the hallways, bearing the cripples away.

It seems especially bitter to me to have fallen for all that stuff after the sensibleness of my childhood. I spent those years enamored of pocket knives and cushioned soled, basketball sneakers. I mooned over cogsoled hiking boots the way I never did over maryjanes. And yet, at some undefined, unspecified time, I allowed my own vision to become distorted. How can I blame poor Isabel for her desire to please when I have the same infection myself?

Pondering on this I move from my spot on the floor and work my way toward the dining room where the drinks are, since that's a goal, a place to go where I can look purposeful. I often drink too much at parties out of boredom and nervousness.

As I make my way now, a woman alone, and unattached to any group, I become seemingly invisible. Men step backward to ease the pressure on their feet and practically step on me. The women I might talk to are all busily talking to men and keep their eyes fixed, seemingly mesmerized, on their faces.

I stir my drink with my finger, sip, and try not to look desperate. Desperation scares human beings as much as it does dogs. But then there is a hand on my shoulder, and Victor saying anxiously in my ear, "How do you think it's going? Are people enjoying themselves? You know this is the first party I've given since Olivia left and I hope people aren't whispering behind their hands, 'Oh, poor old Victor! He sure can't cope without Olivia, can he?' "

"It looks like a fine party," I tell him, my anxiety suddenly, magically, disappearing. "Nobody's looking at you funny that I can see."

Victor puts his arm around my shoulder and leans down to whisper in my ear. "There's something I want to show you after a while," he says. "Damndest thing . . . you'll see what I mean."

"All right," I say, hardly breathing. Our heads are touching and I feel that old conspirator's closeness to Victor. We could be the only people in the room.

Later on, I'm sitting on a sofa talking to Diana when Victor appears and motions for me to follow him.

He leads me through the side door and up the stairs.

"What is it, Victor? What've you found?" I ask as we climb, but he only shakes his head and puts his finger to his lips.

I feel strange climbing these stairs again after all these months. There, on the desk on the stair landing is the same book that was lying there in April before Olivia went away. It's a thick book by Lèvi-Strauss that Olivia clearly never got very far into. She liked leaving meaty books lying around to show how much of an intellectual she was. Victor may have been a professor, but she was the one with brains, or so she liked people to think.

Victor opens the door of the bedroom he used to share with

Olivia, and pulls me inside. "What?" I say, feeling uneasy at being suddenly confronted with the kingsized bed and with Victor's slippers half concealed under it. But Victor motions for me to sit on the bed while he opens the drawer to his bedside table and takes out a slim black book, leather bound.

"This," he says, pressing it into my hands. He sits in a chair on the other side of the lamp and watches me as I carefully open to the first page.

It is, I see at a glance, a diary or a journal since on the first page there's a date in the corner. The handwriting I recognize as Olivia's — her small, quick hand. October the 15th is the first entry, a month after Victor and Olivia got to Rome.

> *Met Paolo at the Spanish Steps. Went to his apartment. Knew that this would be the day and so did he. Was trembling so I could hardly wait for the wheezy little lift to get us to the fifth floor. My hand was burning in his and I could see my darling's pulse fairly hammering in his throat. How I wanted to put my lips against that sweet throbbing! As soon as we came through the door we began undressing, a trail of clothes leading right to the bed. And, oh my god, we were frantic by then — he was inside me before we touched the bed — I was full to splitting — I thought I would die, was dying . . . his teeth will leave their perfect mark in my shoulder for a week but I will do something to keep V. from seeing . . .*

In the entry of the following day Paolo and Olivia make love in the bath, in the great old-fashioned bathtub six feet long, Olivia cradled in Paolo's arms and with his sinewy legs — which she describes as being like a god's — encircling her and pulling her onto what both Fanny Hill and Olivia call his "formidable weapon" while Paolo caresses her breasts and whispers in her ear, croons really, "Oh yes, my sweet dear, I will put it all inside you every inch, so slowly, that I will fill your belly, I will caress your belly through the walls of your womb, I will make you sick with love . . ."

My face grew hot and my hands damp though, goodness knows, Olivia is no literary stylist, is too corny even for pornography, though I suppose pornography is always corny.

"Something, isn't it?" Victor says, watching my face as I read.

"Yeah," I say, not knowing what other response I'm supposed to make.

"You look a little flushed. Are you flushed?"

"Am I?" I say, touching my cheeks and feeling them grow hotter. "Too much Scotch, probably . . ."

"Well, what do you think?" Victor says, motioning toward the black book, watching my face.

"It's pretty bad. From a literary point of view."

"Yes it is, isn't it? If Olivia had lived a hundred years ago she'd probably have spent her time lying around on a chaise longue reading Mrs. Gaskell and passing around an autograph book so her friends could write little ditties in it about her eyes being as bright as the gems that bespangle the brow of the night. That kind of thing. But that wasn't what I meant. Why do you think she left a thing like that lying around when she ran off to Rome? Just to torment me? What was she thinking of?"

"I guess," I say uncertainly, "that since she was going over to be with Paolo in person that she didn't have to take along the book too."

"His knotty legs in the flesh better than his knotty legs in imagination . . . well, you're my expert on Olivia these days. But I think she was rubbing it in . . ."

"Oh, Victor, you know Olivia," I say, trying to be comforting. "She forgot the book, if you want to know the real reason. Slipped her mind."

"Obviously I *don't* know Olivia," Victor says, his voice rising. "Not a damned thing, maybe. Everything I look at that book it gives me a jolt, like biting down on a quicky tooth. But hell, Lee, you're a writer. Maybe you can even make use of Olivia's little book some time. It might come in handy for an erotic scene or something. Use it verbatim if you want to. She'd never have the guts to sue you."

"Well, if you're just going to throw it out . . ." I tell him.

"Take it, take it. I needed to show it to somebody and you were the obvious person."

45

The truth is I want the book. I've always been a sucker for mystery and anyway I want to read the rest of it. I have the feeling, no matter how ridiculous, that Olivia wrote it for me, for my instruction and edification.

I once sneaked my father's Masonic book from the knife drawer in the sideboard, but of course what I discovered in its pages was merely deadly dull. Who cared about the Masonic handclasp anyway? I wanted to know the mystery of the universe and all they told me was how to knock on the door so a meeting of Masons would let me in. And of course once they'd seen I was a girl they'd have kicked me out even if I had given the right knock. But Olivia's black book strikes me as being more promising.

On the way home from the party Walter asks what Victor and I were doing upstairs for so long. He doesn't ask suspiciously. It wouldn't have crossed his mind that Victor and I could have been making wild love in one of the spare bedrooms.

"Oh, Victor had found a manuscript of Olivia's, a short story, and he wondered if it was worth keeping," I told him, the lie slipping easily from my tongue. Why upset Walter by the little book that was sliding even now to the bottom of my purse along with all the half unwrapped tampons?

It's easier to lie to Walter than I would have supposed. He just clicks his tongue and smiles, his slow anticipatory smile that means he's going to say something funny. "If you ask me, the only thing Olivia could write would be a Gothic romance. But wouldn't she be furious if she heard me say that?"

"You're right about the Gothic romance part," I tell him. "The story wasn't any good, so I told him to throw it out. Probably he should throw out everything that belonged to Olivia. Get rid of all that stuff and start over. Why should he allow Olivia to go on hurting him every time he sees one of her books lying around?"

"Oh I agree, I agree," Walter says emphatically as though he and I are the kind of people who discard old loves every day of the week with the ease that other people free themselves of yellowed linen and tea pots with broken spouts.

46

5

Deep in the night, when Walter's breath is sliding long and lingeringly from his ribs and parted lips, I cautiously slide from bed, grope in my purse for Olivia's book, and carry it off stealthily to the bathroom where I lock the door and sit on the john seat in my flannel nightgown, my feel cooling against the tiles. I can't wait to get on with the story, to read of Olivia's and Paolo's transports under a full moon in the shadows of the Forum (having bribed the guard), their folded raincoats cushioning them from the rough ground, Olivia taking Paolo's turgid member into — as she put it — the warm silkiness of her mouth, and drinking deeply at the very fountain of his being.

The language was terrible, the scenes banal, but Olivia could keep me reading on — no question about that. On through the scene (back, now, in Paolo's apartment during a hot October afternoon) where Olivia lies *abandoned to pleasure, crucified to joy on Paolo's bed as he leans over me, his hair, as curly as a satyr's, brushing my skin, his tongue a liquid flame of joy curling into that center of my being, licking it to greater and greater ripeness, to unendurable pleasure so I cry, my breath sobs as the flame of his tongue caresses deeper, plunges inside me, a flame that touches every molecule to life, melts into pleasure so great that I writhe, I cry out, become as liquid fire . . .*

I put Olivia's book face down on the floor, and, for some reason, get up and brush my teeth.

Whether she knew it or not, at that time when I used to sit on the stool in Olivia's kitchen, my heels caught over the rungs, sipping my white wine and talking about the meaning of life, I looked to Olivia as mentor, if not as sage. She might ask my advice, she might ask me questions about my view of the world, but this was generosity, only. I was really a know-nothing in comparison with Olivia, and this had nothing to do with brains.

When I sit back down on the john and pick up the black book I'm not sure how he got there, but it's Victor and me I imagine lying on our combined raincoats at one end of the Forum where moonlight lies over our nakedness and the cats' yowling hides my moans as Victor nuzzles my nipples with his tongue.

But of course that's just a fantasy. Anybody can have a fantasy. Fantasies are as common as burdock — everybody has them. Who cares, what difference does it make, if I conjure up a ghostly Victor as a lover?

I have never supposed that it mattered that my lovemaking with Walter has always been staid, lacking in imagination. Does it matter that Walter and I would feel merely silly enacting some scene out of the *Satyricon* where, as I clasped his legs and begged for mercy, he elucidated in titillating detail how he was going to have me flayed? We would flub our lines like high school students trying to perform *King Lear*. Our marriage is too brotherly/sisterly for such extravagances. But I've never supposed it made any difference. We have stayed together in easy contentment while more flamboyant marraiges broke up like paper ships in a stormy sea.

So I go back to the bedroom and stick Olivia's black book into the back of the bottom drawer of my bedside table, under the pages of Felicity's baby book — the book in which I dutifully recorded the date on which Felicity rolled over unaided, the date on which I first noticed the tip of a tooth breaking through the gum.

As September ripens, the trees gathering color, the sun lying warm in a kind of last, fleeting benediction, I sit at the rickety table under the eaves of Victor's farmhouse, and spin out on paper the days of my infancy, of my childhood. The thread unravels slowly leading . . . where? In a direction I am only beginning to glimpse. To see all is to understand all. I am even smug in my ability to part the curtain. A pull on the rope, the pulleys creaking slightly, and the heavy velvet curtains part. There childhood is, the scenes as vivid as dreams, the beginning during which the path was laid out, the terms set. I don't need the aid of a Fassbinder, with his quirky rules and regulations, to guide me as long as I have typewriter and my table with the uneven legs, the only sounds those of the creak on the stairs, the rattling in the walls — as familiar to me after a time as the swish of blood against my eardrums.

Day by day the rest of the rooms in the house are gradually filling with furniture but I see nothing of Victor. Occasionally I use one of his tea bags; once I drink a glass of his wine, but I see no more of him than Beauty sees the Beast though she eats his food and sleeps between his smooth sheets.

And then, one morning when I drive up the road to the house over that mat of leaves so heavy that the tires only make a rustling noise passing over them, I am jolted by the sight of another car, parked under the walnut trees.

I think of fleeing, of abandoning for the day my room under the eaves where the flies buzz groggily into the glass, though I am dismayed by the prospect. I have come to think of it as *my* room, my right to be there assured. And it is, after all, only Victor's car parked under the trees. He can hardly be surprised to see me at his door.

Nevertheless, what I see on Victor's face when he answers my rattle on the screen, is surprise. He has forgotten about me, I see that in an instant. It has slipped his mind completely that I will be coming to his house so early in the morning. But he recovers quickly, pulls back the door and tells me to come in. "Don't just stand there like a cat somebody's dumped on the stoop," is what he says.

And so I step inside and see, with instant dismay, the young woman sitting at the kitchen table, wearing a satiny dressing gown and eyeing me over the top of her coffee cup. *She's* not bothered; I'm the one who looks nonplussed.

Victor busies himself at the stove, pouring me a cup of instant coffee and making the introductions over his shoulder. "Nancy who works in the Bursar's Office" is the woman at the table and I am "an old friend who writes upstairs." His duties accomplished, he makes straight for the stairs and says brusquely, "Leaving the house in ten minutes. Class to get to."

"Oh, I'll be ready," Nancy says, walling her eyes heavenward

49

for my benefit. She's just waiting for Victor to get out of the room so she can lean over the table to say in a stage whisper, "He's just the nicest man, Victor, don't you think? It takes an older man to be really *sweet*. I mean, most of the guys I know are so selfish, really, never thinking about *anybody* but their own little selves."

"I suppose it's a matter of opinion," I say, straddling my chair and blowing on my coffee. Nancy doesn't look much over twenty and she has cowy, eager eyes of the kind I particularly dislike. "I guess his wife must have found some kind of flaw in him."

"Oh, yeah, his wife," Nancy says, nodding vigorously as though she knows all about *that*. Her eyes take on an avid, greedy look. "I'm just dying to know. What did his wife look like? Was she pretty?"

"*Pretty* wouldn't do it," I tell her, laying it on thick. "Beautiful. One of the most beautiful women I've ever seen."

A pouting look comes into Nancy's eyes and she chips at a little crack in her coffee cup with her fingernail. "Well, gee," she says, "but I guess looks aren't everything, are they? She could be beautiful as anything and not very nice."

"Oh, she's nice too," I say quickly. "And Victor was crazy about her. If you ask me, all he's doing now is checking off time. He may never recover completely. You know, of course, that *she* left *him*. Came as an absolute shock. A note under the sugar bowl and she was already in the air on her way to Rome, joining an archaeologist she'd fallen head over heels in love with."

But I've said too much. Sympathy glows immediately in Nancy's eyes like a cigarette lighter flaring on a dark night. "He must've felt just *awful*, coming in the door that night and all the lights off, nothing to eat or anything, and then that little piece of paper under the sugar bowl. She couldn't be very nice to do a thing like that."

I'm still hanging around in the kitchen when Victor and Nancy come through ready to go. In six minutes Nancy has dressed, brushed her hair, managed to put on pale apricot lipstick that shows up her honey colored skin to good advantage. Not a hair out of place.

Victor, it seems to me, avoids my eye as he waves goodbye but

I don't know. Can't tell. All I know is that he puts his arm around her as they run out to the car and I can hear them laughing until the door slams shut.

I feel in a very sour mood when I sit at my writing table under the windows, though, goodness knows, it's no business of mine who Victor chooses to share his bed with. But, for some reason, I remain disgruntled, typing with fury and snatching sheets out of the typewriter as though they are tongues I'm pulling from somebody's head.

For days I stop going to the farmhouse since I don't want to confront Victor and Nancy in another *tête-à-tête* across the breakfast table. But I feel cross and hard-done-by all the same. I try to work at home but I'm reminded, again, of why this is so difficult. Patsy, who ordinarily spends the morning sleeping under our bed, is taken by sudden digestive crises that demand he be let outside now, on the instant, or he can't be held responsible for the consequences. The telephone rings and although I don't answer it during its first plaintive series of rings I decide, when it begins again, that one of the girls has cut her head open on the sidewalk and is being rushed to the hospital, or that Walter has dropped dead in front of his Art of the Western World class. When I give in and answer, of course it's only someone wanting me to collect for the cancer drive or buy a pizza from the Band Boosters, but no matter with what fury I slam down the receiver my concentration is broken and I must gather the shattered threads of my thoughts about me again, an effort that costs more and more as the morning advances.

The weather, which has been so fine, turns sullen. Clouds cover the sky and cold rain falls, carrying the leaves even before they've reached their prime into sodden heaps that children kick their way through on the way to school.

Everyone I know seems to be in a bad mood.

Diana has gotten sick — again — of Elliot and decides that she can't bear another morning of seeing Elliot's toothbrush lying in a white puddle on the edge of the washbasin.

I come in her door one afternoon and see her striding up and

51

down, looking furious, something held as evidence in her outstretched hand. "Look at that!" she says, and drops the evidence into the wastebasket. A small heap of bent pipe cleaners.

"Maybe he just forgot," I say, feeling depressed. Everyone seems to be going through an upheaval of some kind or other.

"Like hell he forgot," Diana says, hands on hips, eyes blazing. She's just been waiting for an excuse, I know it, and know, too, that nothing will save Elliot now.

"It's not the first thing," Diana says. "Twice now I've found his soggy towels on the bathroom floor and on Sunday he ate lunch when I wasn't here and left the dishes in the sink. So that's it. Kaput."

She hands me a paper sack and tells me to empty the top drawer of the bureau into it while she looks through the dirty clothes for stray socks.

I see as soon as I open the drawer that Elliot never settled with much confidence into Diana's life. All he has in his drawer are toothbrush, toothpaste, Prell concentrate and Arid Extra-Dry, all in the smallest sizes.

Diana is like a hog rooting for truffles, triumphant at finding further evidence of how Elliot has taken advantage of her good nature. "Aha!" she says, extracting a maroon and brown striped tie from the closet.

She holds up a pair of grimy white socks which she pulls from under the bed with as much pleasure as though they were the murder weapon, and starts in on the refrigerator, piling Elliot's meager belongings on the kitchen table. A carton of yogurt, a half empty bottle of wine. Diana puts everything into a heap and loops the tie like a coiled snake around the whole and stands back to observe the effect.

"Well, that's it. Let's celebrate."

She carefully extricates the wine from the pile, pours two glasses, and we sit, one on either side of Elliot's belongings, to make merry.

Our good mood evaporates, though, even before we've emptied our glasses. I see moodiness coming over Diana like fog rolling in from the sea.

52

"Everytime I do something like this I feel mean, but what can I do? I can't stand him around any longer: I couldn't take the kind of thing you have with Walter."

"Ummm," I say, running my finger around the rim of my glass until it hums, a pure, sweet sound. "Did you know that Victor has something going with some girl in the Bursar's Office?"

"No, no, not the Bursar's Office. She's a musician who lives out of town. A flutist. I saw them together in the Lamplighter Room the other night."

I shrug my shoulders and pour myself another glass of wine.

In the nights the rain falls, the leaves, half green, half yellow, cling to the tree limbs, stuck there like something a child slaps down with a hand.

I am restless and dig Olivia's black book out of my drawer once more. Even as I sit under the humming fluorescent lamp in the bathroom, straining my eyes, my feet turning to ice, I tell myself to cut it out, to go to bed, no good can come of it. But I have to continue that romance which is as enticing as one of those pastries displayed under glass, the kind with a violet of sugar stuck onto the top which leaves your teeth gritty and your stomach heavy after you've eaten it. But I go on to the last page where Olivia, packing to return home with Victor, says that never, never can she give up Paolo, her Priapus, her curly headed satyr. Her heart is full of black despair, her body a dry and raging desert without the water of his love.

When I finally climb back into bed beside Walter his hand reaches for mine even in his sleep. He wants us to huddle together, I know, in our old familiar babes-in-the-woods pose, the dangers of the night banished outside our closed embrace.

Then one morning, when I have dropped off the girls at nursery school, I turn the nose of the car out of town. I don't care if Victor is having breakfast with Nancy, the flutist, or the whole of some women's orchestra. All I have to do is say good morning, march up the stairs, and shut the door.

So when I rattle the screen door of the farmhouse, my collar turned up against the rain, my face is set. Ready, I suppose, for anything.

The only person sitting at the kitchen table, however, is Victor, wearing a terrycloth robe with pulled threads and looking at this hour of the morning somewhat haggard. He brightens when he sees me, though, and gets up to pull out a chair. "Good lord! On a day like this," is what he says. "I thought you'd abandoned me and my nice little room."

I stand, dripping, uncertain whether to venture further into the room or not but he says, "Sit. Pour yourself some coffee and cheer me up."

"I thought maybe you'd have somebody with you," I say, and Victor makes a grimace as though he'd bitten down on a green persimmon.

"I suppose all those loose tongues out there have been wagging away, huh?"

"You know it only takes one person seeing you go in the Lamplighter Room with a pretty girl. You know we have to take our entertainment where we find it."

I pour myself a cup of coffee and sit down on the other side of the table from him. A position, however, that I'm instantly sorry about since Victor props one elbow on the table and rests his chin on his hand, fixing me with those honey colored eyes of his. I forget, when I'm not with Victor, how he tends to stare.

"The bachelor life is overrated if you ask me. I've had my fling, but I think I'm going to subside for awhile."

"Olivia told me once that you'd end up with some woman twenty years younger than her."

"Did she really?" Victor shakes his head doubtfully. "Funny, funny."

A silence falls between us and I fiddle with my coffee cup, turning it in little half circles on the table. I'm aware that between the edges of Victor's robe I can see black curly hair sprouting and I keep reminding myself to turn my eyes in some different direction. I am aware, though I try to ignore the knowledge, that Victor is still studying my face as though there is some clue that he is searching for. The questioning, sizing up look he's giving me

54

makes me distinctly uneasy and I lower my eyes from his and keep them resolutely on my cup.

"Lee?" he says, and touches my hand across the table. I have some premonition of what he wants to say to me, and at that moment I give my cup too hard a shove and coffee sloshes onto the table. "Oh damn," I say and hurry to get a tea towel to mop up the spill. Victor leaps up, too, to help me, and somehow we fall against each other. We come together and spring apart again as though we've been stung.

"Let me, let me," Victor says urgently, trying to wrest the towel from my hand, but I hang on too and there we are, stumbling against each other again though, as far as I know, our conscious intent was to avoid touching again.

"Oh, sorry," Victor says, and this time manages to take the towel from my hand. He mops up the coffee, pours me a fresh cup, and we sit, leaning across the table toward each other.

But then the unthinkable occurs. It's terrible, too embarrassing for words, but the moment I sit my hand reaches out in some spastic movement that appears to take place without any volition of mine, and there goes my coffee again, right into my lap.

With little cries we spring up once more, we grab once more for the towel and again, like actors going through a seemingly spontaneous collision that is, in fact, as carefully orchestrated as a dance, we fall together once more. This time, giving in to what seems to be inevitability, Victor puts his arm around my shoulder and holds me as he pats my lap with the already damp towel. I lean against him as I did that far off time in Dean Stacks' hallway.

I know of only one instance of a similar thing happening to me. Once, when I was a freshman in college, I accepted an invitation to go folk dancing with a lanky boy from my Western Civilization class. I didn't find him particularly attractive but what the hell. It was only a Saturday night dance in the Union. However, there was another boy there whom my eyes lighted on as soon as I came in the door. I could not, in fact, take my eyes from his face, and mysteriously, no matter what the formal designs of the dance which took me weaving in and out all around the room or bobbing back and forth stooping for the oyster, digging for the clam, when it was time to grab partners I always found myself directly in front of this boy. My feet carried me unbidden, unfailingly to his side. Even when I saw the downright nervousness with which he looked up and saw me yet again, bereft of partner, standing in front of him, I was unable to prevent the peculiar drift that carried me straight to his side.

The same thing, as far as I can make out, which carries Walter's thoughts, no matter how wide their sweep into the unknown, unerringly as homing pigeons to the particular thing he would like to keep hidden in his sessions with Fassbinder.

"I'm so sorry," I say, near tears. "I don't know what's wrong with me . . ."

Victor pulls my head against his chest and rocks me in his arms. "It isn't just you. I feel the same way."

"But I'm getting you all wet," I say in agitation, trying to pull away but he only holds me closer and kisses me on the ear, on the cheek, finally on the mouth.

"Lee?" he says, taking my hand and pulling me behind him, "let's go upstairs."

My jeans are so clammy against my legs I have to walk bowlegged.

"We'll soon have them off . . ." he says.

I don't think, don't consider. I seem to have known all along that this was going to be what would happen. We have been working out for weeks the elaborate movements that would make this appear inevitable, so that the audience would see only spontaneity in our performance. Anyone could see that this was the way it had to be.

Beginning and Beyond

Beginning at the beginning, then, with the bright light in that oily little room in the Kellam Hospital where, hanging upside down like a pear on a limb, I blinked my eyes at the dim shapes swimming in and out of my vision. They could swim, so why couldn't I? I waved arms and legs, trying, but had lost the skill — the first unfair thing — and I was beached forever on that lumpy white landscape I could see under me stretched out like a map, while I hung by my feet. My mother saying in a weak voice, "A girl? With that jaw and that nose? Lord! Are you sure?"

"Ha, ha," said the doctor, a dapper little man with a pointed grey beard and a limp that swayed me — trough and wave — to my mother's belly which waited for me like an unmade bed. "Use your eyes, Hettie."

And with his fingers, as thick as German sausages, he exposed the tiny pink bud, stunted before it had gotten a good start in life, like one of those inscriptions on the gravestones of infants in Mt. Hope Cemetery — *Budded on Earth to Bloom in Heaven*.

"Well, I know I shouldn't be too picky," my mother said bravely. "But why in the world she has to be given George's looks I'll never know. Just look at Olson, now, with those curls like an angel."

That evening I got the chance to since Olson and my father came to the hospital to welcome me into this world.

I lay, replete on nothing but air, and looked into the curious faces of my family bent over my white wicker basket, hanging like moons over my face and disappearing again, of no more interest to me at that moment than the shapes of the shadows of leaves rippling over the walls. It was six o'clock on a May evening, and outside the hospital window the Paul's Scarlet Climbers were in full bloom.

My brother Olson of the angelic curls — a tall boy of over two — leaned over my basket and stared at me with eyes like the sky. Then one of his fingers reached out, lightning fast, and jabbed me in the stomach when no one was looking. When I cried he took my chilly, skinny foot in his hand with a trip like a trap.

There was my father with his long awl shaped chin and thin nose which spread out unexpectedly at the tip like a spot of ink on a blotter. I should have taken warning looking up into his homely, foolish face with the sandy hair plastered flat over one ear. But the dice were already thrown and there seemed nothing to do but go through with it.

My father gave me a vague smile as though he were afraid I was an acquaintance he should be able to greet by a name which had completely slipped his mind.

"Well, what do you think about her, George?" my mother asked from the bed.

"I can't remember Olson looking so shriveled up. Though perhaps he did."

"No. And he wasn't bald, either. She's got your nose. Have you noticed?"

"Oh lord, I hope not," my father said in justifiable consternation. He leaned over, inches from my face, but whatever he saw evidently didn't ease him much.

"Don't you think she'll grow up to look like you?" he said hopefully.

My mother maintained a discrete silence.

"The poor little grasshopper," my father said, giving me a guilty look.

*   *   *

Although my father was going to go on calling me Poor Little Grasshopper — *Hoppy* for short — I had a name, Margaret Lee, picked out months in advance by my mother. She intended all along to call me Maggie — a name I was going to grow up hating. It made me think of *nag* and *maggot* and *saggy*, and I passionately wanted, early on, to be called Lee. In imagination I was never anything but Lee — the fastest, bravest, strongest. A spy behind

58

enemy lines. Like a good spy I came, in time, to see things I wasn't meant to see.

In the light of the lamp Mother is holding Olson on her lap. He is lolling into the curve of her arm with his head bent a little like a flower on a stem I might have thought but probably didn't since poetic thoughts of flowers on stems don't usually occur to those whose insides are being slowly corroded away—like an old battery left to the rain—by the acid of jealousy. His head just fit into the hollow of her shoulder. With what tenderness she held him, one arm like a belt across his stomach and one hand resting on his bare thigh. He was wearing nothing but shorts, his long legs reaching nearly to the floor, his toes hanging lower than his heels, his high arches (flared like thoroughbred horses' nostrils) rubbing gently against her legs. They fit together perfectly like pieces of the same puzzle. Although they did not say a word I could feel the flow of understanding between them. Their eyes, looking absently toward the lamp as though into fire, were identical.

I had never been held like that in my life and never would be. Small wonder that I wanted to outdo Olson, or *be* Olson, for that matter. Oh yes, I would have been delirious with happiness to have slid into the skin of his body, shaking out his curls over my head.

My mother, being frugal, dressed me in Olson's outgrown clothes. So, hands deep in my pockets, I tagged along behind Olson, imitating his walk, imitating the way he flung his head back at intervals to clear the curls out of his eyes, learning to be a good copy. In the soft, worn cloth of my brother's pants I felt along my skin what his skin had felt; walking behind him in the dust of the road in front of our house I squashed his footprints with my own, looking anxiously at his brown shoulders in case he should turn around and see that I was erasing him off the face of the earth. But although he saw what I was doing he didn't understand; he had the gentle good nature of one who has never had to struggle for his heart's dearest wishes. Why was he so favored? Naturally, or maybe not naturally at all, I suspected the little wand between his legs.

I watched anxiously over my own little bud, encouraging it to grow. There was nothing wrong with it that I could see. I felt both protective of it and saddened by its diminutiveness——*Tom Thumb* was one of my favorite stories. Swallowing my pride, one day, I asked Olson how he had gotten his to grow. Giving me one of his wide-eyed, mildly puzzled looks, he only shook his head. "I dunno. Can't remember."

"Well, look ahere."

I pulled down my shorts and we bent our heads over my shy little bud——it was hardly a strange sight to Olson since we took baths together two or three times a week——but we had never applied ourselves to the problem I presented us with before. "Why do you reckon it won't grow?"

Olson frowned, squatting in the dust on his heels.

"I dunno. Maybe you ought to stretch it out."

So I kept stretching, though the deep narrow pockets in Olson's hand-me-down trousers, and, from time to time, when we were in private, we compared.

"It's getting longer," Olson said every time.

"I dunno," I said. "I must not be doing something right."

Mother thought it was cute the way I trailed around after Olson, wearing his clothes like an undersized Charlie Chaplin, imitating him in word and gesture. She would call her friends to look——members of the Sewing Club or Home Demonstration Club——so that the front windows of the house would be full of gently bobbing heads, all grinning at the sight of me solemnly duckwalking down the sidewalk behind Olson, holding my ankles in my hands.

In the weeds behind the chicken house, I practiced peeing standing up. If I leaned back with my legs wide spread and peed with all my force, the thin little stream would arc nearly as far as Olson could shoot his, but without his accuracy.

"My sister can pee like a boy," Olson bragged to the boy down the road——Warren Hunter——who was six.

"Bet she can't."

"Wadda you bet?"

Warren turned out his pockets. A battered top was what Olson held out for.

"Okay," Warren said shrewdly. "For your wagon."

He was an ugly, flat faced boy with pig eyes.

"Momma won't let you," I said, but Olson interrupted me, plunging madly ahead.

"Deal!" he said.

We all trooped, single file, to the far side of Warren's family's garden. The okra shut us from sight of the house.

Wasting no time I undid my suspenders and leaned back.

But with legs spread, back arched, and with Warren and Olson standing a respectful distance away, I realized something was wrong.

"I don't have to do a pee."

"She can't do it!" Warren chortled. "I won!"

"Go in the house and get a drink," Olson said, giving me a furious look. "A big drink."

I drank so much water that I gurgled, trotting back to our stand behind the okra stalks.

"Okay," Olson said. "Stand back! Here she comes."

Again I unfastened suspenders and leaned back. I could feel it coming this time and heady with excitement, sure of certain success, I held it back letting the suspense build up.

When I let go it was a dandy, going right over the top of a tomato vine without grazing a leaf and making a dark circle in the dirt on the other side.

"Boy! Look at that!" Olson said. "Your sister can't do that. Not another girl in this whole town could do that!"

I was highly impressed—not another girl in the town—I was awed by my own glory.

"That's not nothing!" Warren said, his pig eyes gleaming. In a trice he'd unzipped and sent a thick stream over two tomato plants.

"We win," Olson said, standing his ground. "You have to give us the top."

"Who's going to make me?"

With a squeal Warren was off through the corn.

But we pinned him up against the Kentucky wonder beans and he threw the top into the heavy grass in the empty lot between our houses.

Olson and I spent the afternoon looking for it but we never found it.

*　　*　　*

Did I really think that I could grow myself a prick from the humble beginnings I possessed and be another boy child rocked on my mother's knee? Alas, the question was never as simple as that. I wanted to be a boy, all right, but I also wanted to be the right kind of girl. But there's the rub. The *right* kind of girl. Beautiful, like my mother. Here's where the whole question takes on ambiguity.

There I am dressed to the teeth for Sunday School one tulipy spring Sunday, wearing a white organdy dress with small blue flowers and a shiny blue sash. I have on white silky stockings that reach up well past my ankles and which set off my black shiny Roman sandals. They are new. In fact everything I'm wearing is new so it must be Easter Sunday.

The night before Mother had put up my straight hair in rag curlers and now she has me standing in front of the long mirror in her bedroom untying the long strips of soft rag which releases my hair in long, thin coils. My hair is so fine and straight that as soon as they are released my curls look like coils which have lost their spring. Nevertheless, my mother brushes each curl around her finger with a baby brush. "Oh, you're going to look so pretty I'll bet you won't even know yourself." She bends over my head, breathing moist breath over each curl so it will cling to her finger.

I am trusting and not unwilling to be made beautiful. Not at all unwilling. But, looking in the mirror, I see what is happening. My face — long, thin, with rounded chin and high forehead — is not transformed at all by the silly mop of straw colored curls that hang, limply, down my cheeks and which are held by the gay little barrettes in the shape of bows. I am not pretty, not even after the pain — and I would be willing to suffer for beauty — of sleeping in the hard knobs the rags made.

Not one to brood when I could act, I grabbed the brush where my mother had imprudently set it down, and threw it against the baseboard where it whirled around.

If I'd been pretty — and amiable and sweet tempered and good natured as a result — my mother and I would have had one of

62

those nice, cozy, giggly, sisterly kinds of things going where we would have spent hours doing up each other's hair and trying dresses on for each other and going off arm in arm shopping, and all that.

Of course I was a disappointment to my mother. But she put up a good front to her friends.

"Looks aren't everything," she would say, bravely, while her Sewing Club friends bent over their smocking and bit off thread with their teeth. Snip, snip. A noise as decisive as wire cutters. "I'd much rather Maggie had a good head on her shoulders than be just another pretty face. I'd rather my children were *good* than anything else."

The Sewing Club ladies set up a hum of approval, like a hive of contented bees. "Oh my yes. Isn't that the way to look at it now."

Of course they didn't really mean it.

They crowded around my brother Allen's bassinet a few months later, gooing and cooing, passing him around from one to the other as though he were a piece of fine glass. My mother had him dolled up in a long white dress and with his olive skin and silky brown hair he was the epitome of the beautiful baby.

"Look at that little rosebud mouth."

"Oh, I could eat you up you little sweetheart, yes I could!"

Rest assured they'd never found me as delectable as all that.

I spent a lot of time in the backyard squatting in the dirt drawing magic circles with baby eyes (two dots) and a grin which I would then obliterate with vicious slashes of my stick. Sometimes I attached a fat bug body with spidery arms and legs and prick. Then I would get rid of the whole thing, leaving the ground a hatched up mess.

Now my mother had two of them — one for each arm, each leg, each hollowed out shoulder bone. Sweet, beautiful little children with properly grown pricks and rounded knees smooth as butter that just fit the curve of her hands.

Standing in the doorway — feet widespread like Henry VIII, elbows jutting out like table corners — I looked twisting swords into all three.

63

"Come on, sweetheart. There's room for one more," my mother said, smiling her cat smile.

I only frowned more deeply than ever and said I didn't want to.

No wonder my brothers could look back at me from Mother's lap with mild eyes as sweet as calves'. Weren't they there rocked in the bosom, not of Abraham (all those paternal bosoms always struck me as being false jobs) but of the earth mother herself from which all good things flow? Just let me try to wade in on some of that milk and honey and all of a sudden it was a dry river bed. Tough titty for Maggie.

It just didn't work out in our family the way it was supposed to with fathers. Little girl, disappointed by the incomplete love she gets from momma turns to daddy for solace, or at least that's what we've been led to believe should happen. So why didn't this neat little pattern — so satisfying for all — work out in the Stuart family? Where was my father all those years when I was engaged in that awesome struggle to take my mother away from my brothers, or at least to stake out a claim, no matter how modest?

He was where he usually was — in the Kellam Hardware uncrating mohair sofas and keeping the five penny nails separate from the two penny nails.

Sometimes I spent afternoons in the hardware, playing in the storeroom with old packing crates. I made a hide-out in one of them — my hide-out behind enemy lines. I had little in my packing crate hide-out except a yellow tablet — the kind that had an Indian chief on the cover — and a pencil cut in a neat checker-board pattern with a pocket knife I stole from the display case on the counter. I had four knives — all stolen — but the one with the pearly handle was my favorite.

I spent long afternoons with the yellow tablet pressed against my knobby knees writing adventure stories about a man named Billy who lived in a log cabin in the wilderness:

Billy shut the door of the cabin behind him and went off in the woods to look for something to eat. Food hadn't passed his lips for two days, and his stomach never quit its hurting. All around him in a circle the wolves howled and on the ground in front of him he spied a bear track! The woods were dark as pitch and Billy staggered on his weak legs . . .

Whenever any one came into the storeroom poking around for a gallon can of cream colored paint or for a couple of two-by-fours, I would whip the tablet under my heap of carpet scraps. What I wrote there was a secret not to be shared even with Olson. Only I would know of the ways of escape from hopeless situations. I never saved Billy until he was at his last gasp, but he was always, somehow, triumphant in the end.

At closing time my father would come to the door of the storeroom and call out the nickname that only he called me by. "Hop—py! Hey, Hoppy!"

Though we walked home together I did not walk sedately, my hand in my father's, as other little girls walked beside their fathers. Instead I galloped up and down in front of him like a yo-yo on a string or walked on the raised curb, balanced by my outstretched arms. My father smiled sweetly if our eyes happened to meet, but mostly he seemed absentminded about me. When he stopped, which was often, to talk to a friend, both of them standing in the middle of the sidewalk for a long, slow exchange of nothing in particular, he seemingly forgot about me. If I went on without him he never seemed to notice. We were too much alike, perhaps, to find each other very exciting. Or maybe it was simply that my father's love for my mother was such that it didn't leave much to spare for anyone else.

On the way home from the hardware, my father often ducked into a store to buy my mother a magazine, a little white sacks of chocolate kisses, a yard of lace to put on a collar—*something*.

In the Pruitt Fabric Shoppe we pore over the thimbles. There is a whole tray of thimbles but we have narrowed the choice down to two—one has a chain of daisies embossed on it and the other a plump robin in flight. Which one would she prefer? I favor the daisies and he seems to favor the bird. We stand for ten minutes, fifteen, our elbows on the counter, considering the merits of each.

At last my father makes a characteristic decision. He will buy them both and keep one until such time as she misplaces the first. All the way home we flip a coin—best out of ten—robin, daisies, robin.

"Of course I love it," Mother says, not very enthusiastically, when she opens the sacks. This is what she always says to my father's gifts. But she can't help adding, "You shouldn't have done it." My father's gifts weigh on her spirit, I think, though for a long time I don't know why.

In the swing, one May evening, my mother sits gently rocking, one arm around Olson, one around Allen. In her lap a book with three heads bent over it. My father, coming up the walk, stops by the rosebush ostensibly to scrape a flattened blob of chewing gum from his shoe but really to look, to feast his eyes on the pretty picture—*Oh Do Read On, Mother Dear*, or, *The Hungry Sheep Look Up*.

Maybe the force with which my father throws the curl of gum into the bushes indicates a spasm of jealousy but I'm not sure. My mother is a smart despot; *she* pretends that my father is the sun which we all circle although not even Allen who is probably four at the time believes this.

"Here comes Daddy, boys," Mother sings out as though *this* is what they've all been waiting for with baited breath for hours. Olson and Allen, dutiful and quick to take a hint, run down the walk screeching, trying to outdo each other in grabbing Daddy's legs and pulling on Daddy's arms. Only I, scowling under the Chinaberry tree, see all three look back to mother for approval. Didn't we do that well? Didn't that look like the real thing?

Mother beamed a smile on all three; she could appreciate a picture too. *Daddy's Home!* or *Best Moment of the Day*.

Only one picture would have interested me: *The Family Hope*. In that one I stand transformed into a handsome young man, facing the open door and looking bravely into the world. Behind me Mother, diminished by some unknown trouble—probably the deaths of all the other family members since the two of us are the only ones to be seen—sits clasping her hands thankfully towards my manly back.

I am the dark horse to watch. I am the one who will, ultimately, in spite of the odds, bring home the bacon.

I set out early to do this.

For one thing, I was smart. I lasted only a week in first grade before I was shifted to second. Before Christmas I was in Olson's grade — third. And I wasn't content to stake out only academics for my own. I hogged in on baseball and running base and marbles and wrestling. It so happened that I was pretty good at all these things — even wrestling — in spite of my skinniness. I could hold up my end because I fought dirty. A sharp knee in the groin was my speciality.

So I was riding high with straight A report cards to drop in my mother's lap every six weeks and with success on the playing fields of the Kellam Grade School. My sense of power reached a kind of peak that early summer when I had just turned eight.

The time? Decoration Day Sunday at the Mt. Hope Cemetery where Mother's folks are buried.

The place? Aunt Babe and Uncle Tobe's house the other side of Silver Creek where we went every year for Decoration.

Decoration was an all day affair starting with picking the flowers in the morning early while the dew was still on them — ruthlessly denuding the iris and the rose bushes of whatever blooms they had left and sticking them into dill pickle jars and lard cans full of water. These would slosh over in the back of the car as we went over the rutted country roads and Olson, Allen and I had to sit on our feet to keep them from getting wet.

Church at the Mt. Hope Freewill Baptist — Aunt Babe and Uncle Tobe's church. Mother spaced us out — Olson, Daddy, Allen, herself, me — like the layers in a club sandwich, so we children couldn't squabble and punch each other with our elbows and force each other to drop our collection plate nickels onto the floor. All we could do was to sit and slowly stick to the pews with the glue of our own sweat.

And even surviving the sermon didn't leave us to a much happier fate. The grownups then had to greet each other and talk for a prescribed amount of time under the skinny, sickly looking pine trees while we children stood in catatonic stupors watching the big, vicious looking black ants scrounging around on the rocky ground.

Then slowly, still talking, the grownups all moved off to cars and trucks and brought out the flowers which were already the worse for wear — the iris maybe holding up pretty well but the roses already bending limply on their stems like chickens with rubber necks.

Another interminable time of putting flowers on graves, we children parceling them out the way we would deal a deck of cards.

But the actual depositing of flowers in the sunken peanut butter jars which contained just enough water to keep the flowers from dying in front of our eyes, though the whole point of Decoration Day, did not, by any manner of means, release us from it.

Next there was an enormous dinner at Aunt Babe's and Uncle Tobe's, and then the worst part of the day stretched before us, hot and terrible.

We children have changed out of Sunday best and into old clothes by this time and are finally set free but this is a hollow victory. Olson, Allen, and I now have nerve wracking hours to get through somehow with our second counsins, the Ledbetter boys. There are three of them and when I'm eight they are ten, nine, and six — John Ronald, Billy Joe, and Manning. They have long, skinny hillbilly faces and gaps between their teeth, and they hate us because we live in town and read books. They can hardly read at all and count on their fingers. We would be glad to have nothing to do with them, but no, the Ledbetters are driven to seek us out wherever we might try to hide ourselves so they can prove to us once again how much better they are than we. The criteria for this game, needless to say, is set by the Ledbetters. Because they are good ole country boys and are fearless and shrewd as a result, they will pick up snakes with their bare hands, go into a pasture with a bull, and take eggs from setting hens. Our fear, disgust, and loathing in the face of these challenges mark us as being lilylivered, chicken hearted, useless members of the intelligentsia. They, on the other hand, are the salt of the earth, workers of the world, noble savages.

Their favorite way of showing their superiority was by terrorizing us.

When Allen was three they shut him in a pen with a blind rooster which listened for your movements and would unerringly run for you if you so much as breathed loudly, and once he reached you he would flog your legs with his spurs and beak. Shut up with this rooster Allen stood petrified for seconds while the rooster cocked his head and walked in a drunken circle. But then Allen lost his nerve and started screaming and trying to climb the wire and the rooster, flapping his wings and crowing, barreled across the pen and began taking little chunks out of Allen's legs.

Their daddy beat the hell out of the Ledbetter boys with his belt while they howled and danced — we watched this performance with our mouths open, our heathen hearts warmed by the cries of our enemies — but it didn't do any good.

The next year they shut all three of us in the brooder house and said they were sending snakes in the drain pipes. We stood, our backs together in the middle of the dim, creepy room where the dampness activated the ancient smell of what the Ledbetters called "chicken squat" and stared at the dark circles of the drain pipes until our eyes felt strained. We didn't have anything to defend ourselves with and nothing to climb on and, again, only our cries — shameful, we knew it — brought the grownups to our rescue.

This year, though, I was ready for them. I had sharpened my pearly handled knife the night before until I could shave the hairs off my arm. I told Olson to bring his knife too. Allen was too little to have a knife so we would have to take his defense into our own hands.

The Ledbetters barely let us finish our angel food cake before they were there in a row in front of us, grinning like hound dogs. They'd gotten their hair shaved off for summer and their ears stuck out like lichen on a stump.

"We got somethin to show yew," John Ronald said, dancing

up and down in his excitement. They said the very same thing every year, not even having the imagination to think up a new ploy. We would have said we didn't want to see whatever it was if we'd thought it would have done us any good; we knew it wouldn't.

So we set off behind the Ledbetters who danced on ahead, beside themselves with glee. Just so, devilish little pygmies led the missionaries to the poisoned spears in the forest.

"J'all ever see a snake nest?" John Ronald said, looking over his shoulder at us. We were climbing the hill behind Uncle Tobe's house, the hill where the big rocks stood.

"No, and we don't want to either," Olson said.

"Oh, these here's not even hatched out yit. You aren't scared of a bunch of little ole *eggs* are you?"

We allowed as how we weren't.

To get to the snake nest we had to climb to the top of one of the big boulders. On the other side, in a pit between rocks, the eager Ledbetters pointed out the nest. We, however, couldn't see anything but a pile of leaves.

Naturally not.

To see we would have to lean over the edge of the rock. While we were leaning over, intent on looking, the Ledbetters would push us into the fissure between the rocks where the baby snakes — probably rattlesnakes — would already have hatched under the leaves. The Ledbetters, of course, would guard the steep sides of the rocks keeping us frantic at the bottom.

John Ronald was lying spread eagle on the rock, so intent on showing us where to look that he had forgotten any possibility of his own danger. And, admittedly, we'd never given him much to worry about before.

Quietly I opened the biggest blade on my knife, crept even with John Ronald's shoulders, and leaped. I got him well between the knees, before he knew what was what and although he twisted around so he was facing me it didn't do him any good. I pressed my knuckles into his Adam's apple and held up the knife so he could see it.

"Sit on Billy Joe," I yelled to Olson, who promptly did.

I knew Allen wouldn't be any match for Manning, but I fixed Manning's plow by flashing the knife in his face and yelling to him I would cut open his brother's gizzard if he made a move. Allen, to do him credit, took hold of Manning's ankle and held on — not a very useful move but one that showed that he wasn't a complete pansy anyway, even if he was only five.

John Ronald was squirming under my seat, so it was like sitting on a warm, moist fish, but he didn't try very hard to roll me off. For one thing, I had his arms pinned under my knees and his air supply about half cut off with my fist, and for another his guilty conscience made him think that I really might cut him open and gut him like a catfish.

I liked having his body pinned down under my legs; a sweet curl of pleasure rose from that part of my anatomy now firmly pressing John Ronald's rib cage against the rock.

It went to my head, that wonderful sense of power, and I realized what bullies saw in this game. I bounced up and down on John Ronald's ribs which made him grunt with every bounce in short gasps. But this wasn't enough. I was nearly at a pinnacle of mean joy and I wanted to do something to him that would set my mark on him for good.

"Hey, Olson," I said — bounce, bounce — "I think I'll cut his pecker off. That'll give him something to think about."

Olson laughed a little weakly; he didn't know how much I was joking. Whether I was joking. I didn't know either. But there was a practical matter. I did know that I couldn't turn my attention from the front part of John Ronald to the back part without losing control, so John Ronald's pecker was probably safe enough.

I had to content myself with toying with him, slipping my blade into the sleeve of his tee shirt and cutting the material straight across.

Billy Joe let out a wail. I think he thought his brother's skin was going to be next.

And I did trace the tip of the knife over John Ronald's bony breastbone. Power had certainly gone to my head. However, the trouble with power is that even it becomes a little wearing after awhile. Boring even. You have to keep upping the ante or the steam goes out of it. So I couldn't sit there for the rest of the afternoon bouncing up and down on John Ronald's ribs and making him grunt. I didn't want to carry the thing into the ground.

So, with one quick movement I released the top half of John Ronald and got in a good upper cut in the groin with my knee at the same time — a blow that sent him doubled up to the bottom of the rock. Olson got off Billy Joe and Allen turned loose of Manning's ankle. As we walked off — cocksure and victorious — Billy Joe yelled that they'd get us now for sure.

They came up a little later, swinging their arms like soldiers, their faces grimly triumphant, to the grownups—the men to be exact — who were sitting around under the black walnut trees.

"Maggie sat on top of John Ronald and cut up his shirt with that knife of hers. Amin to cut out his gizzard," Billy Joe announced in a loud voice, giving us a mean, satisfied look.

The men all stopped talking, their faces growing light with this diversion.

"She *what?*" Uncle Tobe said. Everyone except the Ledbetters caught the playacting note in his voice.

"She sat on top of John Ronald and choked him and said she was fixin to cut im open."

"You don't say! She really have a knife in her hand?"

The Ledbetters nodded vigorously, their eyes wide with righteous indignation.

Olson, Allen, and I, sitting in the bed of Uncle Tobe's pickup, could see what was coming a mile off but the Ledbetters were too dense.

"Now what I want to know," Uncle Tobe said in his slow drawl, "is how she got up there in the first place?"

"She jumped on im from behind," Manning said. "She didn give him no chance a-tall."

"He was taken back by a girl two years younger than him, huh?" Uncle Tobe said musingly. "Well, I don't know as I would want anything as mean as that sitting on my stomach neither. Maybe we ought to trade her off to the Marines. Reckon that's what we ought to do?"

The men suddenly let out the guffaws they'd been holding

back, and in the pickup we stamped our feet. The Ledbetters were reduced to scraping their toes along the ground.

Victory was sweet! Oh, how sweet! I was so full of myself I couldn't stand it and had to climb the slats to the top of the pickup, throw back my head, and yell to let off steam. The world was mine. I knew it.

If only I could have held onto that feeling.

But that, alas, was not to be. If I could triumph I could also be defeated, and I was to find that out before too long a time.

* * *

When school started again I continued to join Olson and his friends at recess in games of baseball and running base and red rover. I was chosen early when we were separating into teams and I was generally singled out for favors—a bite off a Babe Ruth if anybody had one to offer, or a few chews on a blob of chewing gum before all the sweet was chewed out.

Still, sometimes I would unaccountably fall from grace and favor. I would detect a certain sullenness when I joined the boys around the marble ring, or they would rudely elbow me out of the good positions when we were playing running base. These moods didn't usually have any discernible cause; they happened just as changes in the weather happened. Disfavor was in the air and could light, like rain, on any of our heads. But disfavor was particularly hard for me to take because I would be forced to see, then, on what thin ice I always treaded. I could be demoted and sent back to the girls at a moment's notice.

The important thing was not to lose face when this happened. So for days I would play with the girls and pretend to like it; I wouldn't give the boys a glance.

Not that the girls wanted me, exactly. I was a tomboy and a traitor, after all, but I had a few partisans who wouldn't let me be cast into the limbo of having no one to play with. Missionary types, they had a certain zeal in showing me the error of my ways. They whooped it up when I was around to show how much more fun the girls had than the boys.

When I played with the girls they seemed to go in for games like rotten egg. They could really get me with that one. In rotten

73

egg the egg clasps arms tightly around her legs. Then two other girls pick up the egg under the armpits, swinging her back and forth saying this incantation: One, two, three, out goes you, you old dirty dish rag you!

At *you* the egg is tossed forward into the grass where, if she lands doubled up arms still around legs, she is dubbed a good egg. But if she comes apart — which I usually did — she is a bad egg and the others jump around holding their noses and yelling, "Rotten egg! Rotten egg! Phew!" Until the rotten egg gets to its feet and starts running, chased by all the others — their fat faces oily with excitement — singing out, "Go home! And wash your face with buttermilk! And read the Bible nine times!" The magic formula for turning bad eggs into good eggs.

Who wouldn't prefer baseball and running base?

After days of rotten egg, and of being cornered in the girls' restroom by long faced girls with small shiny eyes who warned me that their mommas all said I wouldn't ever find a man to marry me if I went on playing with the boys the way I did — I would know, somehow, one morning, that the cloud had lifted from my head and had lit on someone else's, and it would be okay for me to join the boys at recess again.

I supposed, in my simple ignorance, that things would continue like this forever; even when I found myself more and more often in disfavor I went ahead with my customary optimism. I was still allowed to play — most of the time — with the boys I had always played with but I was teased more and more by other boys, especially by the older sixth grade ones who seemingly had nothing better to do than to chase me around the schoolyard at recess yelling "Tomboy! Tomboy! Tomboy!"

Sometimes I yelled back at them, "Shove it up your behinds, you jackasses," but that was just what they wanted, to get me on the defensive, so one day I tried a new tactic.

Dodging back and forth behind the flagpole, trying to escape a ragged string of sixth grade boys, I yelled, "I know something you don't know. I'm just as much a boy as any of you are!"

I didn't expect the stir my words caused. The boys may have been waiting for weeks for me to say this very thing because as soon

74

as the fateful words passed my lips their arms went up automatically—as though they were all giving the Nazi salute—and they
pointed their fingers at me at once.

"She says she's a boy!" they cried, beside themselves with
delight.

I knew from the first moment that I had made a mistake. A
bad mistake.

I knew there was a plan afoot concerning me, but I
went—stiff backed and brave—through the day aware of whispering behind my shoulders, of guffawing, of pointed fingers. I
even knew, through some peculiar second sight, what plan it was
they were hatching up. I felt the trap closing down but didn't
know how to spring it.

But no, that isn't quite true. The myth of my own invicibility
was the spring that shut that trap down with a clang. I could
handle it all myself; I was Lee the Unconquerable who would
always elude anything that the villains could throw my way.

Ordinarily I walked home after school with Olson, but on
that afternoon Olson had basketball practice and I was too proud to
wait around for him, just as I was too proud to change the route I
usually took from school. I could have scampered home like a
scared mouse, cutting down back streets and maybe swinging all
the way out into the fields and pastures behind the town. But no. I
had to march out like the member of some doomed clan at
Culloden into the withering English fire.

I even knew where the ambush would lie in wait for
me—just past the corner where I turned up my own street. On
one side of this street there were houses set sparsely. On the other
there were woods, and the boys would be waiting for me in the
deep ditch by the culvert on the woods side of the street. It was the
only place.

As soon as I passed the corner I saw heads bobbing over the
edge of the ditch but I walked on resolutely, not even turning my
head when I heard scrambling in the ditch and running footsteps
crossing the street.

Our actual confrontation was so blurred by the speed with
which they grabbed me that I felt dazed. I knew they were carrying

me like a sack of flour held by the corners, but the trees, seemingly whirling above my head, looked strange. It was only then — in the hands of the enemy so to speak — that I realized that there was such a thing as being overpowered. That turn and twist and bite as I would that five is better than one. It's a lot more fun being the victor than it is being the victim; it didn't take me long to discover this truth.

When they put me on the ground, still holding onto arms and legs, we were a long way from the street and they were breathing hard from the run through the woods — and probably from something else too, and they were laughing a lot in loud, nervous guffaws.

"Okay. Pull im off her, boys," one of them — a big ugly boy with warts on his hands — said.

They all joined in in pulling my jeans and pants from my wildly kicking legs. Not a slack moment in the excitement to that point. They threw my clothes on top of a thorn bush and hung onto my ankles.

"Boy, huh?" the one with warts said. "You sure don't look like any boy I ever saw."

They all laughed, but an uneasy note was apparent in their laughter. The sight of my body, bare as a plucked chicken's, filled them with uneasiness. Silence threatened.

"Kisser," the warty boy said, solving the dilemma. He gave one of the others a great shove between the shoulder blades.

"Aw," that one said, turning red, and pushed another in my direction.

Time out while they all pushed and shoved. Finally one of them took a big breath and suddenly fastened wet soft lips onto mine. And then of course all of them had to, testing nerve and mettle.

"Kisser, kisser, kisser!"

Soft sound of a zipper and something flexible, yet wiry was rubbed over my lips. "Kiss it!" they shouted, voices hoarse from this pinnacle of excitement. "Kiss it, kiss it!"

"Learned your lesson? Say it, say it! *I've learned my lesson.*"

What lesson?

This, I suppose. You're nothing but an uppity
_____. (Fill in the blank with the appropriate word.)
And you better not be uppity any more or next time we'll
_____. (Fill in with the appropriate punishment.)

"Say it, say it!"

"It."

"Say, *I've learned my lesson.*"

"Lesson," I said between clenched teeth.

That was, apparently, enough.

They galloped away in a moment, wheeling like a flock of birds, wild on excitement and power. "And don't you forget it."

What?

Well, yes, okay, I knew. It was this, in fact, which filled me with wild rage and shame and humiliation.

I could be crushed, humiliated and left powerless all — or so it seemed to me — because I was in this bad position of being a girl. But I wasn't a boy and couldn't get the power I needed in that way. I would have to find another — a more subtle, less obvious way to avoid being sent out half-cocked into the world.

6

Sitting on the edge of Victor's bed, my coffee wet jeans lying in a sodden heap on the floor, I have my thumbs hooked in my pants preparatory to sliding them down my legs but I'm stuck with sudden fear and remain that way — Lot's wife turned to salt. This isn't in the script, I know. Nothing in the black book about sudden fear between the ride up on the wheezy elevator and the wild unclothing toward Paolo's bed.

Behind me, his head propped on the pillow, Victor is waiting, running the heel of his hand slowly down my backbone.

"Victor?"

"Um?" he says, slipping his hand around my stomach and pulling me to him across the bed.

"I don't know if I want to or not," I say, turning loose of my pants in order to grab the edge of the bed.

"This is a fine time to think of it," he says in mock disgust, putting his hands around my breasts.

There I am again, ten feet from the top of the gymnasium, paralyzed with fear. I can't stay where I am, obviously—already my legs are trembling and my hands slick with sweat — and if I fall I'll probably kill myself. "Don't you think we should talk more about this before we do it?"

"You're crazy," Victor says, kissing my neck. "This is hardly the time for a philosophical discussion."

"I don't even know what you like. I only know Walter and he's probably peculiar and not like anybody else and I'll make a fool . . ."

"Will you just shut up, Lee? Will you kindly keep your mouth shut and just come here?"

"And I won't be any good, either. I don't think I'm much

good at this kind of thing. Walter and I have never put much stock
. . ."

"Not another word," he says, putting his finger on my mouth.

So I shut up and slide down against Victor's body where I have wanted to be all along.

The odd thing is that as soon as we begin making love I seem to know exactly what he wants and he knows what I want. We fall into that trance of rising desire in which our hands and mouths can make no mistake. It's a curious thing because this is exactly the way I understand Walter's mind, but our bodies have always been standoffish with each other—shy, and if one can use the word without sounding silly—virginal.

But I seem to know all about Victor's body even though, where Walter is soft and smooth, Victor is thin, taut, knobby—even his ribs with their hard ridges dig into mine as though they too would like to enter—hands, mouths, prick and cunt all mediums to some impossible but perfect union, to some all encompassing engulfment. Our cries scare the squirrels away from their scampering over the roof—from the noises we are making we could be suffering terrible pain, we could be dying. Then, when it seems we cannot—when it seems we will hover on the brink forever—we slip over the edge into a blank mindlessness where, for many minutes, we don't hear anything.

After a long time I come to, lying in the tangle of sheets exhausted, sweaty, my skin rubbed sore, blinking at the sunlight and the patterns on the ceiling like someone emerging into light after many deep dreams.

A crow calls, and another. That is the only sound and it seems both very near and very far away. I listen to it as intently as though I expect to hear a message in those raucous cries.

Victor pulls himself up slowly on one elbow and he, too, looks dazed toward the light as though it is a totally unexpected sight. His hair is plastered wildly across his forehead and cheek like the hair clinging to the skin of someone recently drowned. I know that I too must look mad, as the Dionysian revelers were said to

79

have looked on the second day of the rite. He leans over to stare at my face and I look at the fine lines at the corners of his mouth, at the flecks of gold in his eyes, with the same intensity that I studied the faces of Isabel and Felicity when I saw them for the first time while I lay on the delivery table, dazed then, too, by the light and by the sense that something momentous had just happened.

After a few seconds we look shyly away from each other's eyes.

"That was something, wasn't it?" Victor says, breaking the silence and I say yes, it sure was. When we laugh it's the same kind of laugh as when I was in grade school and somebody batted the ball right into the privet at the side of the high school — a home run for sure.

"Was it ever like that with Walter?" Victor asks though he knows the answer before I give it. He says it was never like that with Olivia, either.

"And you thought you wouldn't be any good," he says, giving me a little dig in the ribs. "Just how good do you want to be?"

"But how come? I don't understand . . . Walter and I are so close, and I thought closeness was supposed to be everything . . ."

Victor pushes himself up on the pillows and puts his hands under his head deciding, I know, on a good and edifying answer as he would try to answer a bright student in a seminar. "Remember, how many kinds of love there are—between men and women and mother and child and God and man. The Greeks, you know, had several categories of love . . ."

But I put my hand over his mouth. I don't want a forty minute lecture on the Greek categories of love.

"Victor," I say shyly, "was I really any good?"

He laughs, kisses me, laughs again. "You just want to hear me say it again, don't you? You're just like Kate when she was five. She'd bring me a drawing of a house or some fool thing and I'd assure her it was great. Beyond doubt the best drawing of a house ever produced by a five-year-old. And she'd beam and dance off but three minutes later back she'd come wanting to know if I *really* liked it."

He puts his hands on my shoulders and looks at me solemnly.

"Lee, you were great. We're great together. And no, I don't know how or why and I don't even want to know. I can be grateful without knowing everything about it."

That evening when Walter slams the door behind him and hangs his jacket in the closet, my heart starts beating rapidly and my hand tightens around the wooden spoon I'm stirring a cheese sauce with, the spoon which has become on the instant a stage prop.

As Walter comes into the kitchen, I bend over the saucepan, staring as intently at the cheese sauce as though it were some magic potion I was brewing up.

I expect, somehow, that Walter will take one look at my face turned so intently to the sauce, and know instantly that I'm hiding something from him.

But he only leans over my shoulder to kiss me on the cheek, to lift the lid on the cauliflower steaming on the back burner.

"Oh good," he says, "You know how I love cauliflower cheese."

Of course I know. The entire meal is a kind of expiation.

I find it surprising that Walter doesn't appear to sense betrayal in the set of my shoulders, in the aversion of my eyes, but he does not. He rolls up his sleeves and sets to work on the dishes in the sink the way he always does. "How was your day?" he asks, as I know he is certain to ask, and I say, as easily as oil sliding over a table, "Oh, pretty good. Nothing special."

As I stir the sauce I steal glances at Walter's shoulders, hunched so he can reach the sink, at the somehow touching quality of his hair which has grown down into his collar and is starting to curl, the way it does when it gets longer than he likes to wear it. Hair of that color — sandy red — doesn't usually curl, and I like his hair long, but he feels that it gets in his way.

Somehow it makes me sad that Walter is so easily deceived, that he is so trusting. And yet it seems ridiculous for me to describe what happened in the bed in the farmhouse as *deception* as, in fact, anything Walter should be concerned about. Here I am, after all, in the same easy companionability we share all our evenings. And,

81

anyway, I don't have such a strong sense of what passes for reality for me to feel that there is any difference in my summoning up a ghostly lover with which to share Olivia's and Paolo's ecstatic couplings, and that of adding, as an extra element, the actual texture of skin to the fantasy.

If I'd merely dreamed the hour I spent in Victor's bed — if, lying beside Walter in the middle of the night I had suddenly wakened to damp effusions released by some dream lover — I would have thought nothing of it. I would only have smiled into the pillow and slid into deeper sleep. So what is the big difference between the dream alone and the dream shared with someone else? Very little difference, I tell myself. Very little indeed. Just a certain languor of the body, or the mark of a fingernail in the flesh — a very little thing. Almost a nothing.

"I think maybe the weather is clearing up," Walter says. "The sun broke through the clouds for a few minutes as I was walking home. Maybe we'll have a fine October after all."

I tell him that I hope so, that I hope the clouds blow away and we have nothing but sun from now on.

"Clouds get me down when they're there every morning, just waiting for you when you open your eyes."

I know, I know all that. I know all about the dark clouds that hung, so often, over Walter's Boston when he was little. I know Walter's hatred of rooms that face north, of his refusal to take a hotel room that doesn't have a window. Walter's life is mine, too. I've got it all in my head somewhere, the parts only a little jumbled. He once told me that he considered me the custodian of all the things that he wants to remember. If Walter ever had a terrible accident that deprived him of his memory, of his knowledge of himself, even, I could furnish him with all he needed to know. I could reconstruct Walter, practically from the seed.

And so I tell myself that I will have no difficulty in living on two different levels; there is no reason at all why one world should intrude on the other.

7

This is not to say that these two worlds are, at all times, equal.

In fact, from the moment I came to after making love with Victor the first time, in that kind of disoriented state one comes into sunlight after spending two hours in darkness looking at pictures on a screen, I knew that I opened my eyes into a world of unusual vividness.

I try to explain this to Victor as we lie one morning, languid and easy, after lovemaking.

But even before I finish talking, Victor starts nodding his head as though he knows all about it, that it's completely explicable and not, even, so extraordinary.

"I remember the first time I was in Florence," he tells me, lying with his hands under his heads, looking at the ceiling. "It was just like that, the way you explained it. I was twenty-two and seeing Europe for the first time. Jolted right out of my head. Everything I saw seemed extraordinary—every stone, even, had that patina that comes from being rubbed by hands for hundreds of years. And I was terribly enamored of the light, too. I wanted to write a paper about the way the quality of light in various Italian cities had affected the painters who lived in them. The light dictated the style—something like that. Impractical notion when you come down to it—how can you describe a quality of light? —but I saw it all so clearly, then, because I was in this ecstatic state. When I saw the Baptistry doors for the first time I just stood there in a trance, looking probably like an idiot. I absolutely *devoured* those doors, they entered my very cells as though they were food . . ."

A far-away, happy look comes over Victor's face and I have to nudge him with my elbow to get him to go on. "Well, then what? You've just devoured the Baptistry doors or whatever and then you probably went on to Santa Maria Novella or someplace. What then?"

Victor sighs. "Well, it just didn't last, of course. I couldn't hang onto that heightened perception. What's that St. John of the Cross says about being swept up to God by the ecstasy of the spirit and drawn back to earth by the weight of the body, or however it goes? After awhile——no more than a couple of weeks I'm afraid——I walked through the streets of Florence and didn't see a thing. Well, that's not quite true, but most of the time I was just thinking about where I was going to eat lunch and worrying about a blister on my heel. The old, mundane world taking over again. You know how it is."

I know that for me the moments of daily life tend to get compressed into a kind of sludge. If my life were revealed to me in pictures, it would be a series of stills, like life in a family photograph album, the unrecorded moments swallowed by darkness, lost to all time.

"Victor," I say in agitation, "I don't want to be like some Florentine street you've walked down too many times."

"What?" Victor says, laughing. "We should come together once every three years or so like the conjunction of two planets? How would we manage that? Would we put our hands in front of our eyes every time our paths crossed so we wouldn't become too familiar to each other? Can you really see that working?"

He puts his arm around me and pulls me over to his side and I laugh, but I'm not satisfied all the same.

"And even if we really did do that," he says, becoming more serious, "even if we just got together very occasionally, do you know what would happen?"

I shake my head, though in fact I think I do know.

"We'd have been together so many times in imagination that when we did come together——every six months, say——that it couldn't be as exciting and satisfying as what we'd imagined during all those days we were carefully refraining."

"So we're doomed either way, looks like. Dailiness is going to catch up with us, one way or the other . . ."

"Oh, maybe not," Victor says, rolling over on his side and

propping himself on one elbow so he can look in my face. "Maybe this will be the exception to the rule. The fates won't notice us up here in our room and we can stay on, happy lotus-eaters. Anyway we don't have to think about it. Not right now." He touches my breast with his finger, circling it round and around as my nipple contracts and grows erect with pleasure.

"I love it when you put your head back, just a little, the way you are now. And there go your eyes, shutting like a cat's." He touches the tip of my nipple, bends down his head so he can stroke it with his tongue, and my breath shudders in my throat. "I love to bring that look of lust to your face."

Now he runs his hands down, sliding along my breasts and belly, over and over, keeping me waiting, making me long for it, letting me thrust against his hands as I feel him grow hard against my thigh. I am rolling my head from side to side, involuntary cries coming from my throat, before he eases my legs apart, and slowly comes inside me.

And again, for a time, we are aware only of the vivid moment.

Twice in the same week, as I'm cutting across the campus, I see Victor and Walter walking leisurely down the quad together, their briefcases swinging against their knees. I don't like seeing them together like that although, of course, there's no reason why they shouldn't be. They've always gotten along well—in the factions and splits that periodically disrupt departments even as small as art history, they are invariably on the same side though I happen to know that each has reservations about the other. Walter considers Victor's seemingly endless books about Jacopo Bernini and his ilk to be glitter without much substance. "Same old stuff over and over." And Victor thinks of Walter as a dull plodder. Solid maybe, but tedious. Victor wouldn't give squat for the whole of American painting anyway, and certainly not for the 19th century landscape painters—Asher B. Durand, George Inness, Thomas Doughty—though they are Walter's speciality. So the two of them have remained friends by avoiding discussion of the main thing they have in common.

85

Of, at least, the thing they know and can acknowledge they have in common.

As I watch them ambling along with the falling leaves swirling in their parth — Victor smart in navy blue blazer with silver buttons, stylish blue and white shirt and tie, and Walter, inches taller, in corduroy trousers sprung at the knees and a turtleneck sweater a little stretched in the neck — I have fantasies about what they're talking about. Me, of course. I put myself firmly between them, the center of their thoughts. "So what did you try out on Monday, anway," Walter asks, in this most unlikely of all conversations taking place in my head. "Anything new? Anything you ought to let me in on?"

"Oh, nothing that unusual. Pretty standard stuff. You may have tried it before. The one where you're both kneeling over the edge of the bed and you come in from behind, you reach around to her breasts . . ."

Or:

"She's so unusual, don't you think?" Victor is saying. "You wouldn't think it, or at least it surprised me, to find that under the gawky exterior there's such fire, such inventiveness . . . ?"

But what could poor Walter answer to that? He could only look bewildered and say "Lee?" in a surprised voice.

So their voices cease abruptly even before Victor and Walter disappear together into the Fine Arts building.

Of course Victor and I see each other at parties. That's inevitable since Hanover is no more than a moderate sized town and the faculty is forced to turn to itself for entertainment. Everybody has to go to the annual cocktail party in the Faculty Club in October. It's the party where everyone is eyeing Julie Krause's familiar green maternity smock, the one everybody hoped had been donated to the Salvation Army. The Krause's already have five children — enough for even a fanatic to childbearing, as Julie is. But she goes around looking happily oblivious to the horrified and even angry looks other people are giving her.

"You'd think she'd never heard of the population explosion," Shirley Wilson hisses in my ear. She's one of the faculty gossips, a thin, brown, leathery looking woman whose face has shrunk from her teeth so that she looks like a malicious little monkey. "What makes her think that the rest of us want the world full of little Krauses? It's so selfish."

"Well, Julie's a good mother," I say, nibbling on an olive and looking around as surreptitiously as I can, for Victor.

"What I wonder is what she's going to do when the children grow up and don't need her anymore," Shirley says darkly.

"She'll be so old by that time it probably won't matter," I say, edging away. I've spotted Victor on the other side of the hors d'oeuvres and I make my way to him with as much art as a dancer crossing a stage.

However, when I reach him, my plate in one hand and a drink in the other, I remember to make the smile I give him prudent. I try to get the hang of how I used to stand with Victor at parties, my weight balanced on the leg I eased backwards, my drink thrust like a barrier in front of my chest, smiling a pained little smile while I prepared to retreat. But I can't do it any longer.

Victor grins like the Cheshire cat and bends over to whisper in my ear. "Why don't we sneak off together? Twenty minutes in the coat closet. How about it?"

"If you're not careful I'm not going to even talk to you, Victor," I tell him, giving a quick look around to see if anybody has noticed us.

"You don't think I'm being discreet?" Victor says and affects a stiff, stuffed-shirt pose, one elbow propped against the wall. He tips his head down in that same stiff way, but when his mouth is close enough to my ear to whisper — quick as a frog flicking a fly into its mouth — he slides his tongue along the swirls of my ear.

"Cut it out!" I tell him as I look around in fear and alarm. Nobody seems to be looking in our direction but you can never tell. People may be taking subliminal notice after all — just let them see us together, giggling, and looking furtive at another party or two and they will link us together without even knowing how the knowledge came to them. They'll think, for sure, that they were told the tale by Shirley Wilson.

Victor leans back, letting his face go bland as an oyster, and says in a low, intense tone of voice, "After a long and tedious party the Dean's good wife, having done her duty, and looking forward to television by the fire, is searching around the coats for her fur when she is arrested by some movement in the dim shadows at the back of the coat closet. Not one to be made timid by what she doesn't understand, Janice Stack suddenly parts the coats with a deceptively powerful lunge of the arm. But what she sees leaves the poor woman transfixed with horror, gasping and groping blindly for the coat rail." Victor pauses dramatically and I put my finger to my lips, but he continues anyway. "What Janice Stack sees at the back of the coat closet is nearly too shocking to be related, ladies and gentlemen. All the unwritten laws of decency and good manners are positively flouted before that worthy woman's eyes. Even as she watches, too paralyzed, even, to swing the coats together again, the two naked bodies in the dim recesses behind the furs begin thrusting against each other, faster and faster. A curious cry, unlike any which poor Janice has ever heard before, breaks from the woman's parted lips . . ."

"Oh for heaven's sake, shut up!" I say, just as Walter comes up amiably, smiling his sweet smile, and says, "What's this? What am I missing?"

Not a thing, I tell him. Just a story of Victor's that wasn't even funny.

8

Though I should have been prepared for it, would have been, probably, if I hadn't spent so much of my life in a fog, the problem that I'm confronted with on a cold October night when Walter turns out the light and scoots to my side of the bed, is not one I'd either expected or, therefore, feared.

There I am with Walter in the opening bars of our quiet lovemaking, and for all the pleasure I feel I might as well be a burned saucepan Walter is scrubbing. I shut my eyes and pretend as I try to conjure up Victor's ghostly presence, but my body won't be fooled. It insists there's some major difference between fantasy and reality that I have ignored, or remained in ignorance of. My body has grown used to pleasure greater than Walter's plodding hands can possibly awaken and it won't be satisfied by ghostly presences that can't even breathe in my ear.

Desperate, willing to try anything, I pull Paolo from his warm Roman bed and make him go through his paces but with his best efforts all that he can manage (in a bathtub or quick, quick! in a Tuscan hayfield) is to arouse a feeble excitement that, unaccountably, flattens out to nothing almost as soon as it begins.

"Too tired?" Walter says. "Maybe tonight's no good."

'No, no, it's okay," I say through clenched teeth. "Just don't pay any attention to me."

I could, perhaps, fake it, but decide not to. I won't deceive Walter to his face; if he ever asked me point blank if I were having an affair with Victor I'd have to say yes. I wouldn't lie. And I won't lie about this, either.

But my efforts, though great, are in vain. No go. A fat zero. I tell Walter that it doesn't matter, that these things happen sometimes, that they're mysterious at best and Walter says yes, yes, of course, but his eyes rest on me worriedly, all the same. Within its narrow limits our lovemaking has usually worked.

Walter moves back to his side of the bed, turns on the light, and starts reading. So I turn on my light too and pick up *Emma* from the floor where I'd left her the night before. Of course I've read *Emma* before — ages ago when I was an undergraduate taking 19th century British Literature. I liked it okay when I read it but couldn't get as excited about it as my teacher, Dr. Curzon, did. "But of course you're too young for Jane Austen," he'd confided to me after class one day. "Eighteen? My dear girl, you can't know anything at eighteen. Come back to Jane Austen in ten years and you'll see what I mean. You'll appreciate things then that you can't possibly see now. Or," he'd added darkly, giving me a hard look over the top of his glasses, "maybe you'd better make that fifteen years."

So I'm compromising at twelve; in the ways that count I seem to be a slow learner. And, yes, I have to admit that I see more in *Emma* now than I did at eighteen, though whether or not I see what Dr. Curzon intended I don't know. This time when I read *Emma* I'm annoyed by how neat it all seems — how it is implied that nothing, except for minor domestic quarrels, will mar the tranquility of that oh so happy marriage between Emma and John Knightley. But what I want to know, the scene I'd like to read, is the one after Emma and John have been married for, say, ten years or so. All that sensibleness might pall after a time, mightn't it? John is twenty years older than Emma, after all, and — let's face it — stodgy to boot. What if, after those ten years, a young doctor just Emma's age comes to the village and when one of her children gets whopping cough or croup or measles the young doctor comes to the house? Comes, in fact, repeatedly, even after the child has roses in his cheeks again and is demanding meat for his dinner. If Emma and the young doctor fall madly in love, what then? Would kind, knowing, always *right* Mr. Knightley be any match for the handsome, sensitive doctor? I'll bet he wouldn't. Marriage never was the end of the trail — not even in the 19th century — as Jane Austen would have us believe.

For awhile Walter and I do nothing except turn pages though our reading styles are different. He eases each page over, holding it suspended in air as he reads the last word, whereas I slap my pages over like a pianist roaring through a fast passage.

"Oh, Lee, I'm sorry," Walter says suddenly, putting his book face down over his stomach. "It's all my fault I know. I've been moody for days. But I'm having this perfectly awful time with Fassbinder right now. It's a quarrel, really. One of those deadlocks. Stuff about my parents' marriage keeps coming up and Fassbinder has this bee in his bonnet that my mother had a lover. Maybe several. Nina! Can you see that? Don't you think it's totally absurd?"

"What's so absurd about it?"

I keep my eyes on my book, automatically zipping off the sentences.

"Why should you care if Nina had a lover?"

"But she didn't have one!" Walter says, getting upset. "That's what Fassbinder just won't see. She'd have told me, apart from anything else."

"Any woman *might* have a lover, Walter. It's always possible, you know."

"Can you really imagine Nina having a love affair?"

"Oh, I don't know . . ."

"You know you can't. She just couldn't have kept something like that from me. We were too close. And don't give me that superior smile, either. We just liked the same things. I was an only child. What could be more natural?"

"Nobody said it wasn't *natural*, Walter, given the nature of families. Isn't that what Freud said, or something?"

"And she wasn't possessive, either. She loved you from the first time she met you. In fact she'd have been very upset if we *hadn't* gotten married."

"I know that. I love Nina too."

"It's the secrecy I couldn't have stood."

"Oh, for heaven's sake, Walter! She just might not have considered it any of your business whether or not she had a lover.

Why should she explain all that to a seven-year-old kid? Don't be a dope. The point is that you wanted to be in first place with Nina. Right there in the catbird seat."

"I could read her like a book."

I fix my eyes on the ceiling and keep them there.

"If I hadn't learned through her how to be close to a woman, then we could never have had the kind of marriage we have, could we?"

"No. Probably not," I say, giving the ceiling my full attention.

"What am I going to do about Walter?" I ask Victor the next time we're together at the farmhouse. The weather has turned colder and there is no sunshine to warm us as we lie spent on Victor's bed. We throw the blankets over us and listen to the frantic scrambling of squirrels over the roof.

"Why must you do anything about Walter?"

"I can't make love with Walter any more. You've ruined me for making love with anybody else."

"Now that's ridiculous," Victor says, holding his watch up to the light. "You could teach Walter a new trick or two."

"It's not a matter of a trick of two! It's everything, and you know it. It would be like taking a child's hands and pressing his fingers through the opening bars of the *Emperor Concerto* when the kid himself had only gotten through Book 4 of the graded lessons. Walter lacks a lot more than the right fingering. *That* just isn't the thing we have together."

"Then maybe you shouldn't *be* together. I don't know. Maybe you should leave Walter and live with me. Ever think of that?"

"Leave Walter? Absolutely not! That's out. And then there're the girls . . . no. Total impossibility."

According to you this morning, Lee, everything's impossible. You can't leave Walter, you can't live with Walter except in celibacy . . ."

"I didn't say that. Of course I'm going on living with Walter . . ."

"Well, then," Victor says, throwing back the blankets and

heading for the bathroom, "I don't see what else there is to say. Do you?"

"But I don't want it to get in a mess. Why can't I just have you *and* Walter?"

"You've just given one reason why it's difficult."

"But I just don't *know* anything, Victor. Other women manage things like this all the time, don't they? So why can't I?"

Through the half open door of the bathroom I can see Victor getting dressed, preparing, I know to face his Renaissance Seminar. He becomes, by the moment, more and more the academic.

"Maturity is largely a myth anyway, don't you think?" He leans over the washbasin to knot his tie and I can see he's deliberating how to answer me best, always the good teacher. "I used to believe my parents were incapable of making a foolish mistake. Mistakes, maybe, but not foolish ones. But of course that's all nonsense. Our fields of expertise are so terribly narrow, after all. Mostly we just bungle along hoping the mistakes we make aren't disastrous ones. How many genuinely wise people would you say you'd known in your life?"

"Not a one as far as I know," I tell him as I put on my jeans and shirt. "But that's not the point, I don't think . . ."

Victor slaps a little shaving lotion on his chin and combs his hair. "Then what is the point as you see it?"

I feel put on the spot like some student asked a question in class which he can't answer.

"I don't know! I just don't want everything to be a problem. Is that childish?"

"Oh probably. Haven't I just said that maturity is only a myth?"

"But what should I *do*?"

Victor leans over me on his way to retrieve watch and keys from his bedside table and gives me a long and thoughtful kiss on the back of my neck.

"Haven't you just answered that yourself? You don't want to *do* anything. Isn't that what you said? You want to continue coming to my bed and you want to continue holding Walter's hand in the night. You're not ready to come to any decision, Lee. All you want to do is spin your wheels a little."

"I hate it when you're so superior . . ."

"You hate it when I'm *right*. At least be honest."

So, okay, he's right. But where does that leave us?

9

In mid-November Walter tells me one morning at breakfast that as a special treat — to celebrate our fifth wedding anniversary — he's reserved a room for two nights at the Pine Tree Inn in Settlers Mills — a quiet and pretty 18th century inn that has been recommended to us over and over by our friends.

Why Walter chooses to tell me this at breakfast, a time of day when serious discussion is impossible in our household, I do not know.

"What?" I say, "When?" as I mop honey from Felicity's lap.

"Could you get Faith Krause to stay? The girls like her don't they?"

"Arrr," Isabel says, opening her mouth in disgust to show half chewed toast. "Old Faith." And Felicity drops her head to one side, walls her eyes to the ceiling, and makes a noise as though she's going to throw up.

"Sure they like her," I tell Walter, ignoring the demonstration. "But do you think we ought to go away . . ."

"We haven't had a night away by ourselves for over a year."

I know exactly what's in Walter's mind — that a couple of nights free of our usual responsibilities will rejuvenate our sex life (what there is of it). I can practically hear Fassbinder's voice making the suggestion. But it's that very hope and expectation that makes me uneasy.

But Walter's the one who's really ambivalent about being away from home, and all that ambivalence comes to the fore on the afternoon we leave. He shows Faith, who has agreed to stay with the girls, the long list of emergency telephone numbers although fifteen minutes before he's already pointed them out to her. As an afterthought he adds Fassbinder's number to the list right after

95

that of the Poison Control Center, although what Fassbinder could do in case of emergency I'm not sure.

But finally at 3:15 we kiss the girls and make it to the car. Walter has horrors of the girls crying hysterically after us, but all they do is wave nonchalantly from the dining room windows. Before we leave the driveway, I can see Felicity turning away from the window demanding, I know very well, the present we have left for just this moment.

"What if they're just pretending to be brave?" Walter says miserably.

"When have you ever known Isabel or Felicity to be self-sacrificing?"

On the contrary, both girls are probably going to be a lot tougher than either Walter or me—they'll grow up thinking we're quaint old things but hopelessly impractical. Still, you can never tell. They have their dangerous adolescences to get through first, and, as I should know, anything can happen to them in those terrible years and probably will. Maybe they'll go all to pieces, losing what good sense they have, concerned only about getting the attention of some lanky basketball player who chews gum out the side of his mouth and stomps on his opponents' toes when no one is looking. I dread already my attempts to think of something pleasantly light but not totally inane to say to those boys that Isabel and Felicity will start bringing to the house in ten years time. I've never had much experience of adolescent boys except for my brothers. Certainly I never brought any boys into the house when I was thirteen though Mother would probably have sacrificed her right hand if she could have seen me, just once, bring the Kellam Lions football captain into our kitchen for a baloney sandwich and a Coke. It wouldn't even have had to be the football captain—a round faced boy who played trombone in the band would have done. Any male between the ages of fifteen and nineteen who had an average quota of intelligence and wasn't hideously deformed would have done. But I had nobody at all and, as I said viciously everytime the subject was broached, would not care to so much as exchange the time of day with any of those jackasses.

I know it was a terrible blow for my mother—so pretty

herself and so charming, president of the PTA and the Wesley Womens' Guild, a member of every women's group the town had to offer—to have a daughter who slouched around in engineer's boots and glared at everybody. Who would not pass the cake when the Past Matrons met at our house although other daughters—their names were legion—did it so graciously and sweetly. All I would do was to place myself ostentatiously and maddeningly in the den where all the women had to come for their coats, reading Beckett in the dim light from the north window and sitting with my feet on the furniture—a position I did not change whatsoever, even to raising my eyes from my book, when the women, struggling to get their arms in the sleeves of their coats, regarded me with consternation and, yes, self-satisfaction. *Their* daughters weren't such handfuls. Lydia Stuart might be pretty and the best cook in town—blessed with a loving and hard working husband and two handsome well-mannered boys—but the chickens had really come home to roost in her daughter and that was a fact.

All my poor mother could do was to try to pass me off as a genius of some kind—an assertion that nobody believed and even if they had the acceptance wouldn't have offered much solace to my mother after all. Because who wants a peculiar genius for a daughter? All the women—my mother included although she could never had admitted this publicly—would much rather have had a daughter who had the boys falling all over her. Who wanted some scrawny girl with a sulky face, who insisted on putting her eyes out reading some book nobody in his right mind would tackle anyway?

Well, I would, that's who, but I was almost certainly not going to be given that chance. Mother should have had Isabel and Felicity for daughters. They would have satisfied each other very well. And I? I should have had myself. I would have gotten along very well with me for a daughter.

But maybe I'm wrong about that. Because although I had shown nothing but the most intense contempt for what the women of Kellam, Arkansas, had considered the ideal woman I must have swallowed some of that old nonsense after all. Not that I cared a bean for the football heroes—no, nothing as simple as that. And yet if I hadn't felt that something was missing as I sat with Beckett propped between me and the women struggling into their coats, I wouldn't have had to glare my disapproval of them so. It's the gaps that get us into trouble, as I've noted before. So there is, I'm pretty sure, a direct though maybe somewhat obscure link between the girl scowling into Beckett and the woman moaning in pleasure between Victor's sheets.

As we drive deeper into the country we sink into our thoughts — melancholy ones it appears. The light, at 4:00, has already turned. Though it's been a sunny day it has been cold and deep shadows of bare trees stretching down the long hillsides.

It's a day very much like the one — five years ago — when, in our last fall in Madison as graduate students, we got married at a Justice of the Peace's. Not that we had intended to get married in that way. We'd talked endlessly about the simple wedding we were going to have at my house in the spring. But, I don't know, the more we talked about it the worse it sounded. The realization finally came to us that marriage — the ceremony at least — was only an embarrassment. The night we realized this we were studying for midterms in Walter's apartment, drinking cocoa with our feet tucked under the sofa cushions. Walter suddenly looked up from his book, as though we'd just held a long conversation on the subject though neither of us had spoken for over an hour, and said, "Why not this Friday night, then? There has to be a Justice of the Peace around here somewhere."

Buoyed up by the solemn importance of it all we telephoned our parents immediately after the seven minute ceremony that was to link us together for life. I telephoned first while Walter stood in the phone booth with me, holding my hand. When my father said "Hel?-lo," on the other end of the line and I heard the old familiar twang, I seemed to have lost my tongue and could say nothing, nearly put the receiver right back on the hook. But then I managed to say, "Guess what?" and blurted out on the instant the whole story. My father, as I remember, only took fright at being the recipient of news so momentous, and didn't say a word to me — all he did was to yell for Mother. She was the one who had to deal with crises.

By the time we finished with our families both Walter and I were shaking like aspens even though nobody had had anything but good things to say. Our mothers were a little disappointed not to have been with us at that important moment in our lives, and our fathers were, I gathered, relieved to be spared the fuss. But certainly nobody said anything that should have made us put our arms around each other and sob, as we did the moment the phone was back on its hook. Walter was the only man in the world, probably, who could have seen as clearly as I did how awful it was to get married. Not to *be* married, exactly. We wanted to be married but the transition from one state to the other was so harrowing that it left us dizzy with fear — free fall before the parachute opened.

We drove off in our tears until we came to a fish restaurant called Anchors Away where we unwisely ate fried oysters. Fried oysters introduced into stomachs that were quivery anyway led to predictable results. The oysters allowed us only to reach a nearby Holiday Inn before they began to churn most unpleasantly in our stomachs. Or perhaps it was less the oysters than it was our distress at having taken a terrible step into the unknown that sent us running, in turn, into the bathroom all night to throw up oysters and everything else we had in our stomachs until we were reduced to dry heaves.

We weren't too sick to see how ridiculous it all was — surely no one had ever spent such a wedding night — but this awareness didn't keep us from being overcome with *angst*. We had deserted our families for each other and through the night had to expiate that betrayal. By early light we fell, at last, to sleep and when we woke at mid-morning we felt weak but absolved.

We looked at each other over the breakfast table (suddenly we were ravenous), held hands under the cloth, and whispered "my wife, my husband" as though these words were mystical in their import. They sent shivers down our spines.

All through that day we kept turning to each other to ask,

"Did you have any idea it would make such a difference, seven minutes in a Justice of the Peace?" and all day we shook our heads in wonder, never tiring of considering the mystery.

The dimly lit stairs in the Pine Tree Inn up which Walter toils with the suitcase curves gracefully upward and delicate spindles connect rail with stair though some of the stairs creak and the carpet is worn.

"I'll bet this place is a firetrap," Walter says as he climbs. "We should've asked for a room on ground level."

"The second floor isn't so high. If we have to we'll jump from the windows."

"I can't feel safe in these old buildings. All that ancient dried out wood. It must be a tinderbox."

Walter doesn't feel safe in any building made by human hand but I don't remind him of this.

While I shake out Walter's suit and my dress, Walter goes through his rituals — checking where the fire escape is and putting his head into the night, letting the cold air in, to see what we'll land on if we're forced to jump from the windows in the middle of the night.

"There's a roof down there," he says in relief.

"A mere roof can't save you," I say meanly. "Face it, Walter. There *is* no safety. We could be wiped out any time and there wouldn't be a thing you could do about it."

Walter is hurt by my attack (I'm supposed to understand his fears and calm him down) and he closes the bathroom door very quietly and stays closeted in there for quite a time.

I kick off my shoes and lie on the bed with my hands under my head. I'm going to have to watch it, I see. Some mean, goading part of myself is stirring to life and is going to have to be curbed.

Walter would be better off if he could snarl back the way Leon, his father, used to do, bringing his hand down like a meat chopper on the table when he was exasperated beyond endurance. Of course Leon's outbursts upset everyone else's digestion but they appeared to aid his own. While the rest of us sat looking at our plates, toying with our meat with the prongs of our forks, Leon was tucking in.

However, when Walter comes out of the bathroom with his face pink and his hair brushed I see that he's determined to hold no grudge. He's going to be cheerful and sweet and he's going to be able to tell Fassbinder on Monday what a good weekend he had.

And I feel remorse, too, which makes me anxious to do the right thing. We go downstairs to the dining room arm in arm, pausing only to smile indulgently at the smokey portraits that hang on the poorly lit walls.

The dining room is sparsely occupied — it's November after all and off season. With so many tables to choose from, Walter and I pick a small cramped one against the wall. It's always our choice to have something to lean against or hide behind. We hate sitting at tables in the middle of restaurants where we feel we're on show.

No sooner are we seated than Walter leans toward me over the candle and whispers, "Now what's the relationship between those two, do you think?"

This is one of our favorite games, and while I give the edge of my attention to the menu — knowing already that I'll choose the special whatever it is — I take surreptitious glances at the well-dressed white haired man sitting with a much younger woman at the table on my right. Though he's reasonably well preserved he's at least sixty and she's not more than twenty-five. They're looking intently down at the candle burning in its glass holder and talking about some subject which appears to make them unhappy. Her hands are in her lap, his on the table where he folds and refolds them together. Clearly he's agitated about something.

"I think they're lovers," I tell Walter after the waitress goes away with our order. "*have* been lovers. He's urging her to marry him and she's uncertain. I think she's probably saying 'I'm very fond of you, Robert, but I'm afraid it wouldn't work out. To marry and all.' He tells her that the difference in their ages isn't anything to worry about since he feels like a man of thirty and all that stuff. He's probably a teacher and she's a graduate student. They've got those kinds of funny, intelligent faces."

But Walter is shaking his head no. "That's not the way I see it at all. I think he's her father and he's trying to talk her out of marrying some dumb kid who lives on his father's money and has already flunked out of three colleges. See the way they both keep looking down at the candle as though they're embarrassed? Now if he were her lover he'd keep looking up at her face. Pleading a little."

I have to admit that this is a good point but I won't give in. "She's embarrassed because she's gotten herself into this silly position and she doesn't know how to get out of it without hurting his feelings. He's like an old dog dribbling apologetically over the carpet."

All of a sudden the professor (?) leans across the table and reaches for the girl's shoulder. She draws away, pushes back her chair and flings her napkin on her plate. "No," she says so loudly we can hear. "Absolutely not." And she's leaving the dining room, her chin high, her elbows punching the air behind her. Lover/father hurries after her, shambling a little in his anxiety like a St. Bernard on a waxed floor.

Later on, in the room where most of the guests of the inn have gathered because of the fireplace which is fast consuming great apple logs, we see the white haired man and the girl again. They're sitting at a small table under the windows playing chess. At least they have the chess board set out in front of them but their attention isn't often focused on it. He reaches across the table, takes her hand, and raises it to his lips. With his eyes on hers, he slips the tips of her fingers into his mouth, a gesture made only between a mother and her baby or between two lovers, and I — though maybe not Walter — see that look, both remote and alert, of lust in her eyes. So we are both wrong, but I nudge Walter in the ribs with my elbow anyway; at least I'm more nearly right than he is.

Walter looks annoyed. He considers himself very perceptive in picking up nuances between people—a kind of Henry James in perceiving subtleties. But, come to think of it, he has a blind spot and it's the same blind spot Henry James had to contend with.

Love relationships, consisting of more than the glance, at least, throw both of them off stride.

The white haired man and his girl leave their game unfinished and go out with their arms around each other's waists, heading for an obvious destination, and Walter and I are left with the canasta players in front of the fire and with old issues of *Yankee* and *Adirondack Life* to keep us company. Pictures of deer and articles explaining how to make your own snow shoes pall almost immediately, so Walter pulls me to my feet and we follow in the steps of the lovers. I wonder, as I climb the creaking stairs behind Walter's back, which room the white haired man and girl are occupying and whether or not they're undressed yet. Does she really *want* to make love with that man who could be her father or even grandfather, or is she just indulging him one more time, having landed herself, through her own good nature, in this uncomfortable position? It's not a scene that arouses me much. Of course Victor *is* older than I am but that hasn't got anything to do with it, as far as I know.

The Pine Tree Inn furnishes twin beds in its bedrooms and when Walter climbs into mine when we turn out the light, we seem to be perilously arranged. Anything but carefully concerted movement will surely land us on the floor.

Walter slides his arm under my shoulder and we hold onto each other like two people in danger of drowning in a strong current. He turns his head to whisper in my ear, "It doesn't matter at all whether or not this is a great performance. We're just going to enjoy ourselves."

"Fassbinder's advice, I assume."

"Listen, Lee, you can't deny that Fassbinder knows a lot. And he's really decent, too. He shook hands with me when I left his office on Thursday and said he hoped we'd have a very pleasant weekend."

"Leering, I suppose."

"Just being perfectly sincere. A little fatherly."

"Oh, fatherly," I sneer. "And I bet you're going to tell old father Fassbinder all about it on Monday. Every little detail."

"If that's what's on my mind. But nothing to worry about, if that's what you're thinking. He's perfectly trustworthy."

"I doubt that anybody is perfectly trustworthy," I tell Walter, but he refrains from rising to the bait.

This conversation has gotten us into our old babes-in-the-woods huddle but does not take us further. If we could just let it go at this—lying together in our narrow, perilous bed like those little Medieval figures pressed together in a bas-relief—then maybe all would be well. This is what we're best at, anyhow—making a warm, comfortable nest and huddling together in it. But at thirty and thirty-four we can't just give up all forms of physical intimacy except huddling together and holding hands. Fassbinder could hardly allow an analysand of his to go through three and a half years of analysis and end up with *that*.

"Well," Walter whispers in my ear, "what do you want me to do?"

I pull back, as far as the confines of the bed will let me, and say in outrage, "What kind of a stupid question is that—what do you want me to do? Use your imagination! How do I know what I want you to do until you try it?"

Even in the dark I can feel Walter looking at me uncertainly. "Well . . ." he says, and clears his throat as though he's preparing to launch into one of his Art of the Western World lectures. He reaches out a tentative hand to my breast and jiggles it as though he thinks a little jiggle may set a motor going. When nothing happens his hand seems to die there.

"If I think about it I can't do a thing. You shouldn't have told me to use my imagination. That's like telling somebody to be creative. It's paralyzing."

"Okay. I shouldn't have said that. Let's wipe that out and start over. Don't think about anything. Just drift. Shut your eyes, maybe."

"No, if you tell me not to think . . . oh, look here. Let's just do it the way we always do only when we get to a place where you want a variation just let me know. How's that?"

"That's fine," I say, and take a secret resolve. I'll pull both

Victor and Paolo into the fray right away, putting them to work as industriously as coal miners. Somehow or other I'll pull it off single-handed, though, in fact, the number of hands both real and imagined I must set to the task makes that turn of phrase ridiculous.

The thing that throws my plan out of whack is that Walter keeps changing his mind. Just when we get a rhythm going that I think I can depend on and start embellishing, Walter uneasily falters and begins yet another variation that I have to try to work in. It's like being on the back of a horse that keeps changing on the instant—if a horse could—from trot to canter to extended trot to walk, all those changes in tempo and rhythm effectively keeping one off balance.

"Is this all right?" Walter keeps saying. "Do you want me to do something else? Whisper in your ear? Come in more slowly? Higher up? You could scoot under me more. I can't hold on forever, but I'll do my best . . ."

"Just keep quiet! Act on instinct."

We're both panting now—not from wild desire but from exhaustion. I feel as though I've run four miles already and there's no end in sight.

"Just . . . go . . . ahead!" I gasp out, but Walter gamely hangs on until he can't any longer at which point with a long sigh, he collapses sideways and there's a soft sticky sound as the film of sweat that has joined us gives way.

After a time, Walter comes to and staggers into the bathroom with his pajamas in his hand. I expect that when he comes out he'll sit on the edge of my bed and we'll have to conduct a long post-mortem on what he did wrong and what I could have done to improve matters and what Fassbinder would have had to say if he'd watched our struggles from the shadows.

But to my surprise he bends over me briefly and kisses me on the cheek. "That wasn't too bad, was it?" he says. "We don't have to be some kind of champions, anyway, do we? Very happy anniversary, darling." And he climbs into bed and goes, almost immediately, to sleep.

At first I'm relieved not to have to review the fiasco in detail, but then I start becoming resentful. I am the one left sleepless with nothing but *Emma* for company. And, as luck would have it, I have just reached the scene of the Boxhall picnic where Emma behaves so badly and is chided by Knightley. I'm in no mood to read of fatherly Knightleys scolding naughty Emmas. Knightley is always so even tempered, wise and *right* and Emma is ambivalent, childish, and, at least at moments, mean spirited. It has to be a man (of course) who points out her weaknesses to her, who helps her see the errors of her ways. Who pointed out Knightley's indiscretions to him, I'd like to know? And would he have listened to anyone who had? Still, like it or not, no matter how many times I read *Emma*, Knightley isn't going to change, nor is Emma. She will always decide that this subdued, sensible love is what she's always wanted.

At two in the morning I have a great urge to shake Walter awake and ask him if he doesn't smell smoke or tell him I've just had a bad dream about the girls being kidnapped by a bad looking man with a black mustache. Why isn't he prowling around as usual, worrying? The answer to that is obvious. He has left a sentinel to keep guard during the watches of the night. That's why. Realizing this I click off my light and curl up, an angry lump, under the covers.

The next morning it's raining, a cold, grey rain that settles heavily on the piles of brown leaves and blackens the trunks of trees. When Walter wishes me good morning I give him a sour look.

"Just what are we going to do in this place in the rain?"

"We'll sit in front of the fire and read. And when we're hungry we'll eat huge meals. Maybe we'll even play a game of checkers."

"Who can read in a roomful of retirees playing canasta?"

"Oh, they won't be playing cards this morning," Walter says, determined to be cheerful; this excursion was his idea, after all, and he feels obliged to defend it.

But when we go into the reception room after breakfast, books under arms, the card players fill two tables and they have stationed themselves right in front of the fire.

"Not on your life," I say, heading immediately for the door.

"We'll find another place."

Walter marches headlong into what proves to be the music room—a long chilly room with a spinet at the far end and an organ—the kind you pump with your feet—near the door. In between, placed at rigid intervals, are chairs and two loveseats covered in slick red silk. I imagine interminable Sunday afternoons in this room of sitting bolt upright, balancing a teacup on one's knees, making conversation with the vicar.

We carry our books to the far end and sit on the loveseat, flanked on one side by the spinet and on the other by a brass umbrella stand holding some dusty plumes. The only other occupants of the room are an elderly couple sitting half concealed by the organ, busying themselves with reading the newspaper.

"I'll bet this is where they used to put the corpses on display in their coffins. Someone could have played the organ softly while friends and relatives came around to view the body."

"Um," is all Walter says. He's pretending to be instantly engrossed in his book.

"Aren't you chilly? It isn't very warm in here."

"Get a sweater," Walter says, not taking his eyes from his book.

"I'm wearing a sweater."

"Get another. Wear a jacket."

"Why not a blanket and sit here like some misplaced Indian?"

"All right, Lee," Walter says, steeliness coming into his voice. "I'm sorry it's cold in here. Just what do you want me to do about it?"

"I know you can't do anything," I tell him, and that statement, too, seems to have overtones.

We subside into books but only briefly.

I can read all the signs—the blood suddenly swelling through my wrists, my eyes slitting the way cats' do when they're getting ready for a fight.

"I didn't sleep very well last night."

"Oh? Why not?"

"I just hate being left sort of high and dry that way. Close to the brink but not over. It puts me all out of kelter."

Walter puts his finger carefully in his book and turns slowly to face me, a pink flush starting up his cheeks, the sure sign of anger that he inherited directly from his father. Already I wish I'd kept my mouth shut but it's too late now.

"And just who's fault is it you're out of kelter? Didn't I try to get you to tell me what to do? I begged you to tell me what you wanted but no, all you would say was that it didn't matter."

"I didn't say it didn't matter! When did I ever say it didn't matter? All I said was to stop being so self-conscious. Act on instinct. Those are my exact words if you remember."

"And how was I supposed to do that when you made me self-conscious? As soon as you said *don't think* you knew perfectly well I wouldn't do anything else but."

"Well, whose fault is that? If after three and a half years with Fassbinder and paying him an absolute fortune you can't even cut loose a little bit . . ."

Walter gives me a look as if to say so *that's* it, is it?

"Oh, I know how much you resent Fassbinder. You make it clear enough. But do you know how childish it is? Instead of accepting him as an ally you've always thought of him as the enemy."

"That's not true! I've been perfectly cordial to him the few times we've come face to face. I don't even know him. I have no opinion of him one way or the other. What I do resent, though, is your telling him every single little thing — dragging him right into . . . well, right into our marriage, for heaven's sake . . ."

The two old people sitting by the organ rustle their newspapers warningly and glare their disapproval but once we've started we're not about to stop for *them*.

"You're jealous of him," Walter says, looking in spite of his flushed cheeks a little pleased. "But why in the name of heaven should you be jealous of Fassbinder of all people?"

"Why not Fassbinder?" I say, laying it on thick now, indulging myself, dumping the blame for everything onto Walter's head. "Every single thing I say to you, everything we do together, is probably going to be passed onto him the next day. You're just a conductor or something . . . a regular little tattle-tale . . ."

"If you want my opinion," Walter says, sounding calm now that I'm the one starting to lose control, "You should go to see him a few times yourself. I think it might prove to be very useful."

"You see?" I say, my voice rising dangerously, "Did you hear that? You sounded exactly like him right then. So pompous. So know it all. And if I went to him too we'd both sound like that. We couldn't even talk except in translation."

"I'll tell you something, Lee. I do think, though you won't like me to say this, that the trouble, you know, in bed we've had recently is a lot more you than it is me. And I should probably tell you that Fassbinder thinks so too. Or at least he's implied . . ."

"Me!" I say, and I am shouting now. "Do you think you and Fassbinder know everything? And there! You've just said it! You *do* tell him everything and what's more the two of you are in cohoots so what do you expect, Walter? Just what do you expect?"

Glaring their disapproval of us and of our unfortunate conversation, the two old people fold their newspapers and stalk out of the room, shutting the door behind them.

For some reason, deprived suddenly of our audience, the wind suddenly goes out of our sails and we fall silent. Walter, who can't stand open dissension for long tries to take my hand but I snatch it away. "I do think," he says, wanting us to get on an even keel again, "that it wouldn't do you any *harm* to pay a visit to Fassbinder. What've you got to lose?"

Plenty, I think.

"Money," I say.

Walter spreads his hands over his knees and shrugs his shoulders. "A few times wouldn't cost that much. But, okay. Only I was wondering what you meant when you asked me what I expected just now. Expect about what?"

"Oh nothing," I answer sullenly. "I don't even know. I was just mad."

We pick up our books and resolutely pass our eyes over the words, but in our heads reverberations continue. We are both the sort to mull and brood though Walter pretends to recover from anger quickly.

109

10

After Walter and I exchanged first memories that night we met at a graduate student party in Madison, we were together nearly every day. At night we walked hand in hand through the snowy streets to the apartment I shared with a crazy girl from Asheville, North Carolina — Gloria — another English major and a poet who wrote her best poetry at two and three in the morning. She went around during the day looking wan and hollow-eyed like a vampire who'd failed to come up with her quota of blood. It was Gloria's theory that a person couldn't write good poetry unless he was out of his mind. Not all the way crazy, maybe, but jolted out of his ordinary, banal habits of thought.

She had a lot of examples to draw from of course — Ezra Pound, John Berryman, Anne Sexton, Robert Lowell — the list of crazy and half crazy poets is very long. And of course there were those like Swinburne who were jolted out of their ordinary minds by drugs, and any number jolted out of *theirs* by alcohol. Even poor old Keats was jolted out of his by fever. I would, apparently, never amount to anything because I liked to eat regularly and needed eight hours of sleep, and, though eccentric, was firmly wedded to my mind.

I was pretty low in Gloria's estimation anyway, and after she met Walter her regard for my abilities as a writer — even potential abilities — sank to a new low. Walter was obviously terribly healthy. One look at his round, guileless face, his Hush Puppies and knitted tie and it was clear to Gloria that he was nothing but walking tedium. "Oh God, an academic!" she said, slapping her forehead with her hand, trying to erase the painful sight of Walter's oxford cloth shirt from her sight. When we were alone, after Walter said goodnight and left, she gave me the full brunt of her warning. "If you *want* to end up in a tract house with wall to wall shag carpeting and three mewling babies in diapers just go ahead and marry him. Go on. But don't say you haven't been warned. Don't say nobody told you. He'll dump you in that hell-hole, too, and go off with his pipe stuck in his teeth to his all important classes and committee meetings because that's the order of the universe as far as he's concerned. Can't you tell by just looking at him?"

I said that Walter's looks were deceiving and he wasn't nearly as conventional as he looked — he didn't even smoke a pipe — but I did not tell Gloria that at Walter's apartment we drank Ovaltine for a nightcap and never carried physical intimacy further than a chaste kiss.

But Gloria had her suspicions. "What do you do in his apartment, anyway?"

"Well, of course we study. And we talk . . ."

"Make love?"

"Not *exactly* . . ."

"I knew it!" Gloria said triumphantly. "I'll bet you never do anything but hold hands. What do you talk about?"

"Oh, philosophy. Art."

I wasn't about to tell Gloria that we talked about our childhoods and our families, that we confided to each other the horror stories of our adolescences.

Walter had been fat and terrible at sports in those crucial years and I had been gawky and blue stocking — both outside the pale. But now we could even rejoice in that pain because it brought the two of us together. It was nothing short of astounding that we had found each other — the soulmates we'd always wanted.

"Recess," I would say in a dreamy voice. "What did you used to do at recess at your school, Walter?"

And he would bring alive for me those terrible game periods where he ran hopelessly and clumsily up and down soccer fields, football fields, his hands turning blue with cold and despair in his heart because he was afraid of the ball and horrified by the savage scramble for it and scared most of all by his coach — a man with a flattened nose and a joint (probably bitten off) missing from one finger. A man who would call "MacDoogal" across a field in such a way that the very syllables have always called up for Walter ever since all that he considered most ridiculous and incompetent about himself. Even now a gurgling sound — the suck of water down a half clogged sink, for instance — reminiscent of "ooo gal" can make his stomach flutter.

Turning lovingly through these relics from our childhoods could keep us going for hours — the storms we have survived, the losses and the terrors and the sweet, ineffable yearnings.

The only thing that bothered me about Walter was a small thing, hardly worth mentioning. From the first time I saw him I thought he had a nice face but a somewhat bland one — not the kind of face I ordinarily found myself staring at. I had never cared too much for that shade of sandy hair that veers on red, and I did not like, either, those red freckles that sprinkled Walter's nose and arms.

Of course I didn't mention this because it would have been unkind. Could Walter *help* the color of his hair? And for all I knew there may have been things he would have liked changed about me, too. He *said* he liked girls with small breasts, but how did I know? We'd both suffered painful adolescences because we were odd looking, so of course we wouldn't make unkind remarks about each other's looks. Looks weren't everything. Looks, in fact, weren't *anything*. Looks, we both insisted, were totally unimportant. And the things that were important, the things we most valued, were the things the two of us had in abundance. We understood each other. That was by far the most important thing.

We understood each other so well, in fact, that Walter never had to ask me to marry him — we just knew all along that that's what we'd do. The only thing left to talk about was how we would live our lives.

Before I met Walter I had never been interested in babies; motherhood, in fact, had always seemed to me definitely unappealing. But, somehow, after I met Walter, I took to staring into the faces of babies I saw being wheeled down sidewalks or held over a shoulder in grocery stores. I even found myself looking with peculiar longing at the displays of baby clothes in shops — at the cunning little sweaters and tiny bootees. My eyes had obviously passed over such objects before, but I had never really seen them.

Now Walter and I spent whole evenings when we should have been taking notes for term papers considering names for our unborn babies. Of course we saw them — those unborn babies — in a totally romantic way, as names attached to cherub bodies, never as cranky two-year-olds having screaming tantrums in the IGA. Walter, who had been an only child, had an excuse for such ignorance. I, who could recall details of Allen's infancy and early childhood perfectly well when I chose to, apparently no longer chose. Whatever babies I had wouldn't be remotely like Allen, anyway. With my children, all would be different.

All would be different about our marriage, too. It would be nothing like our parents' marriages. We would live on a higher plane altogether. It was unthinkable that Walter would ever have me followed by a private detective as Leon had Nina followed, looking for the hordes of lovers the poor woman might have been meeting. Nor would we endure my parents' lopsided marriage — my father adoring my mother in what I could only describe as a self-deceiving way while she treated him as one treats a bigfooted, drooling dog. Lovable, perhaps, but something of a trial to be put up with. I tried to describe for Walter the look of annoyance that used to flick in Mother's eyes when Daddy came up behind her and kissed her on the neck. Her eyes darkened and held a dangerous look for an instant. Then she would step away from my father and say lightly, "Oh, not here, George, for heaven's sake. Why can't you think what you're doing?"

"Why couldn't she just say, 'It annoys me when you kiss me in front of the children?'"

"I think it annoyed her everytime he kissed her, whether the children were around or not. Everytime he kissed her like that it reminded her that he loved her more than she did him. And that made her feel guilty, of course. And because she felt guilty she couldn't say a word. Only show that little flicker of annoyance."

Walter shook his head. "That's really awful, isn't it? Almost worse than my parents where the warfare was a lot more open. I feel a little sorry for both your parents. But, then, who wants to be pitied?"

Nobody would ever have to pity us; we were sure of that. Not as long as we shared everything. And we did, gallantly, try to share all of our past experiences with each other. Walter shared my jealousy when Allen was born; I shared his delight when Leon went away for a business trip and he and Nina were left in peace to play gin rummy and to toast marshmallows in the fireplace. I tagged along on those Sunday afternoon outings when Nina took Walter to the Museum of Fine Arts and stood with him in front of those canvases of Durant or Thomas Cole — those magnificent but dreamlike landscapes more beautiful and noble than any reality could be. Walter was held in thrall by that never-never land. If only he and Nina, holding tightly to each other's hands, could step into that world, to be the only figures in these magnificent landscapes which were mellowed by an evening light which transformed that world of trees and rocks and chasms into a view of paradise glimpsed from afar. Even to be the little figures in Cole's "Expulsion from the Garden of Eden". Of course Walter was bound to be entranced by that glimpse of a perfect world; it thrilled me to see how Walter had discovered his profession. It seemed an inevitable thing, just as our marriage was an inevitable thing.

Walter graduated at a good time — two years before the crunch came in academic jobs — and Hanover University in the middle of New York State, in a town surrounded by woods and low mountains, seemed agreeable to both of us. I got a part-time job teaching freshman composition — a job which would give me time to write. And we bought a tall, skinny house on a corner lot within easy walking distance of the university, where we settled down to the kind of life we'd imagined living when we were graduate students.

It was a way of life made familiar to us by the lives our professors led and nothing about it surprised us. Our car might be old, with strange knocking sounds coming from the carburetor, but our house was full of books and we had two orange crates full of records; we ate well on produce sold at an open market on Saturday mornings by local farmers, and we furnished our house, as everyone expected us to do, from the Salvation Army and used furniture stores.

The first summer after we came to Hanover we spent in Europe, traveling around in a little Fiat and staying in cheap bed and breakfast places. Our lives were practically idyllic, disturbed only by occasional sharp disagreements brought about, or so we said, by having worn ourselves down tramping through too many churches and museums.

In Locarno one afternoon, when we were having tea in a pretty little restaurant overlooking the lake, we had one of these rare quarrels. I looked up from my strawberry tart to see Walter slip his fourth pastry — a thick square covered with a thin skin of dark chocolate — onto his plate. "But those are fifty cents *apiece*, Walter," I cried in outrage. "You've sat right there and eaten up two dollars worth of cakes."

"Have I?" Walter said, looking down at his pastry fork as though he were surprised to find it in his hand. "I wasn't counting, I must say. But after all we can't come to Switzerland for afternoon tea very often, can we?"

"Does that mean you can make a pig of yourself when we do?"

"I hardly think I'm being a *pig*," he said in a stiff voice, his face beginning to flush.

"Look, Walter. Four pastries in one afternoon is enough, don't you think? Unless you're going to go without dinner which I bet you're not. It's so expensive, apart from anything else."

"Two dollars! Three dollars! What's three dollars?" Walter's face went the color of raspberry sherbert. "You wouldn't think twice about spending three dollars on a book, would you? So what's wrong with spending three dollars on a memorable afternoon?"

"A book is permanent. You have it for years. But what's food? Nothing. Gone in a minute."

The real issue, and we both knew it, wasn't over money at all. The real problem was that I didn't want Walter to get fat again as he had been as a child. I would hate it if he grew round jowls and had to waddle as he walked. And it could happen! It could easily happen. Walter's very bones were heavy, or so I imagined — not like mine which were thin and birdlike. I couldn't bear it if Walter's chin started doubling down on his neck and his belly swelled like a toad's. Fat people might be very pleasant and perfectly acceptable members of society but I found fatness physically distasteful. And with his reddish hair and freckles, Walter couldn't afford any further disadvantage.

"That is one of the differences between us," Walter said, carefully scraping a little edge of chocolate onto the side of his fork. "I can enjoy something that only lasts a moment. This wonderful Swiss chocolate, for instance. And you're not really enjoying your strawberry tart at all. It'll take you five years to fully appreciate it and then only in retrospect. You like the *idea* of sitting above Lake Maggiore having afternoon tea more than you enjoy the real thing."

"I do not!" I say, stung. "Who is it who spends his life studying little blobs of paint on canvas? What's that if it's not enjoying life once removed? If anything, I'm the one who gets bogged down in the moment . . ."

"Getting bogged down and seeing isn't the same thing," Walter said, and took a heartier bite of his pastry.

I had to agree that Walter was right. Those two ways of perceiving were not the same. Oh, of course I could look at the lake and the mountains — that scene that Inness would have turned into mystery, the golden light falling on distant peaks like the light falling on John's vision of heaven — but I certainly couldn't live in that light. That ineffable, aching beauty could only be glimpsed, for a moment, from a distance. I wouldn't be able to *see* the scene until I'd separated myself from it; only then would it take on any meaning. Not since childhood, or so it seemed, had I been clearly and wholly engaged in the moment. Ever since (all this seemed as clear as revelation to me as I watched the birds wheel above the lake) I had been deflected from my true purpose by forces which I couldn't yet pinpoint but which were, nevertheless, present like strange unidentified sounds in a dark room.

But then a cloud blew across the sun and the light dimmed; Walter asked if I thought we should go on to Stresa for the night, and I lost the thread of what I was thinking.

116

Back in Hanover that fall our lives continued in their old, pleasant way. Walter began working on a book about George Inness and within two months I placed two stories in literary quarterlies.

Things were going so well that we decided we could slip a baby into the pattern of our lives with hardly a ripple. I would stop teaching, since I had no strong commitment to it anyway, and instead of grading freshman essays I would change the baby's diapers and take it for walks around the block in a well sprung English pram. It seemed a pretty fair exchange, looked at from that vantage point before Isabel was born.

But after she was, of course, the ridiculousness of the exchange became evident. A baby can't be tucked away in a briefcase when you've had enough of it. There it is, twenty-four hours a day, a demanding despot. When Isabel fell into a precarious sleep, Walter and I tiptoed around her crib like people trying to escape from someone holding a gun on us.

Just when I was engrossed in an obsessive way with taking care of Isabel—feeding, changing, bathing her, trying to remember her vitamin C drops and taking her out in the fresh air in her pram — Walter stepped up work on Inness since the drive for tenure had suddenly become a grim business. Academic jobs had dried up, become practically nonexistent.

Yet we continued to share as much as we could. Walter was the one who got up in the night to give Isabel her bottle and to walk up and down with her over his shoulder until she went to sleep again. And at night, after we'd finished the supper dishes together, I went over George Inness with Walter, section by section, paragraph by paragraph, arguing a point here, demanding greater clarity there, turning stilted sentences into clean, simple ones.

We were as close as we had been, or so I thought, though we didn't have as much time to talk about it. We were usually too tired now, to lie awake half the night talking about our childhoods. And even after Leon fell dead with rage that hot day in the Mercedes garage when Isabel was six months old, and Walter saw sudden death coming down on all our heads at any moment, we still shared all these anxieties. I was the one, after all, who encouraged Walter to make that first, terrifying telephone call to Fassbinder, who held his hand, in fact, while he stuttered into the receiver that he thought he wanted an appointment. I was in on it all, and left out of nothing. It had never occurred to me — that the beginning of Walter's tête-à-têtes with Fassbinder three times a week — that of course the stories, which had been only ours, would now be Fassbinder's too. A little wedge, no bigger than the root of a small tree working its way down a fissure in a rock, wormed its way between us. Or maybe that wasn't it at all. Perhaps it wasn't Fassbinder — nor Isabel nor George Inness — nor anything else that hadn't been there in the beginning. A danger which we were too slow witted to be aware of.

11

On the drive back home from Settlers Mills Walter and I don't have much to say. Usually when we're heading for home after being away Walter becomes more and more cheerful the closer we get to home and I sink slowly into depression. But this time Walter's spirits are low, too.

"Penny for your thoughts, Walter."

"Not worth a penny. I was trying to remember whether I left my briefcase with the 19th Century Art quizzes in my office or if I brought it home."

I'm sure that what he's really thinking about is his session tomorrow with Fassbinder, of sinking down on Fassbinder's couch and reliving the weekend—a telling that Walter will find both depressing and satisfying. Voiced aloud, each incident will doubtless form part of a pattern not even glimpsed now. Walter's version though, or the version that he and Fassbinder will make together—that neat bundle—might not even be recognizable to me. I'm the one who may have to wait a long time to realize the true significance of these two days because Walter was right when he told me that it might take me years before I could taste every delectable crumb of that strawberry tart eaten on that long ago afternoon in Locarno.

Right now I'm thinking only with sweet anticipation of running into Victor's farmhouse in the morning and yelling up the stairs, "Hey, I'm back," just as, I imagine, Walter anticipates sinking onto Fassbinder's squashy couch.

In the usual Monday confusion, I don't notice until I see her looking down sadly into her bowl of Rice Chex, that Felicity doesn't seem her usual self. Her cheeks are too pink and she's not bouncing in her chair the way she usually does.

"Eat your cereal, or I'll have to give it to Patsy," I warn her. "Patsy's just waiting."

"Don't want it," Felicity says sadly, and my heart takes a nose-dive. Why this morning of all mornings?

"She looks flushed, don't you think?" Walter says, and I tell him crossly to stop jumping to conclusions. Children often look flushed when they first wake up. However, I don't convince myself with this commonsense wisdom and I'm not at all surprised when I take her temperature to see the silver line resting bluntly, irrevocably, on 101. So that's that. For Felicity a visit to Dr. Swandt and, undoubtedly, the usual pink medicine, and for me the terrible disappointment of not seeing Victor. Felicity will be coddled and played with and spoiled all day; I'm the one I feel sorry for.

Later on, with Walter gone and Felicity and Isabel tucked up on the sofa to watch *Sesame Street*, I telephone Victor to tell him the bad news. After I do there's a moment of silence before he says, "Damn! But I was looking forward so much to seeing you."

"I know, I know, but what can I do?"

"There's nothing you can do, but I don't have to act pleased, do I? I'm disappointed. The day's spoiled . . ."

Even though Victor is only reflecting what I feel myself I'm still, for some reason, annoyed.

"But she does have a temperature, and her throat's sore . . ."

"I don't doubt your word, Lee, for heaven's sake. Don't get neurotic. I'm just sorry you can't come. That's all I'm saying."

Even after I hang up the receiver I feel just a little cross with Victor. *He's* disappointed. Well, what does he think I am? Does he think I arranged the whole thing—Felicity's sore throat and all—just to try his patience, to let him see how much he misses me?

I remember, as I have not for some time, the way he used to stick his head out of his study door when I would be visiting Olivia and say in that peevish voice, "You couldn't have moved the keys for my file from my desk, could you, Livia? I'm certain they were right here."

I wish, in fact, that I could sit on the stool in Olivia's kitchen again, my heels caught on the rungs, my wine glass in my hand, and ask Olivia a few pertinent questions while she sliced onions and chopped peppers.

"What does it mean to 'be in love'?" I'd ask first. "Say that you and Paolo were in one of those either/or situations. Both of you stranded on a little bit of rock which is slowly being engulfed by the incoming tide. And while you're standing there watching the water rise, an old man in a canoe or a kayak pulls up to your rock and offers to save one of you. Only one, mind you. The other would have to stay out there and drown. Would you gladly and even gratefully watch Paolo being rowed to safety as the water rose to your chest? Would you wave with a bright smile on your face? Or would love demand that both of you would have to refuse the old man's offer so you'd drown out there together with your bodies intertwined . . ."

But I don't know. That example may be too extreme, the question may be the wrong one to ask. Probably Olivia would just say, "Love? What's complicated about love? You feel happy when you're with the person you love and desolate when you're not. That's all. That's *it*."

This conversation, even in the fantasy, is becoming unsatisfactory, but I risk one more question, anyway. "But can't you love two people at the same time only in different ways? Look at all the categories of love the Greeks had. I love Walter, I really do, but I don't love him in exactly the same way I love Victor. What you're writing about in your black book — the excitement, the glad joy thing — can't last long, can it? I mean, how can you keep that up with someone you have little quarrels with? Five years from now will Paolo seem any better than Victor? When he can no longer surprise you, how can he thrill you?"

"Oh, for heaven's sake," Olivia would probably say, getting cross. "Do mothers look into the faces of newborn babies and say 'Oh dear. I should never have had you. Think what you're going to be like eighty years from now — decrepit and senile and your neck as scrawny as a rooster's.' If we thought like that all the time we'd never do anything but sit with ashes on our heads and moan. The present moment does count, Lee, whether you choose to believe it or not. Now be a good girl and shift your legs so I can get in that cabinet you're blocking."

Maybe it's impossible to come up with the right question. I imagine suddenly the situation reversed so that I'm the old, experienced wife being questioned by some girl—one of his students, say—who's fallen in love with Walter. I could tell her anything, anything at all about Walter. But with all that wealth of possibility open to her she would probably bend her head to one side—as I'm doing in this confrontation with Olivia—and say, 'Oh my, I just don't know what to ask. There're so many things I'm sure I should, but I just can't think . . . well, but, let me see . . . I have sort of wondered about this thought I know it isn't the least little bit important . . . it's not the kind of thing I should be asking I'm sure but I just wondered . . . which does he like better, a bath or a shower? If he has a preference . . .' "

I know perfectly well that the present moment counts, I tell Olivia. Didn't I open my eyes into a transformed world that first morning Victor and I made love—everything bathed, however briefly, in the light of an Inness painting? Our hands resting on the sheet, the cawing of the crows, taking on a kind of grandeur. The problem being, as it always is, holding onto the wholeness of the moment.

I tell myself that the four days I have Felicity and Isabel home from nursery school should have, if not grandeur, at least a few memorable moments, but even those are hard to achieve.

Whole weeks of ordinary time could fit in those afternoons between the hours of one and four. Some women, or so it seems to me, manage to swim vigorously through days of such tedium but they are heartier than I am. I sink rapidly into a kind of mindlessness.

In this, at least, Walter and I are opposites, since Walter longs, as a saint longs for God, to be allowed to sink into the sweet deadening routines and small daily pleasures and comforts—he wants nothing more than to see every morning the orange juice jug lined with beads of water, the geranium blooming in the window, the napkin folded down the middle and bisecting the plate into

122

even portions. I, however, as these days bring sharply clear to me, am easily buried in the daily trivia, lost in it as in fog.

The only freedom the girls allow me is the limited one of cleaning or cooking. They find bustling movement and noise to be soothing. But if I try to sit down with a book or a writing pad they're on me in a moment, filled with outrage that I should try to escape them in this fashion.

On the fourth day I become cunning. I prop my writing pad against the side of the refrigerator and when they ask me what I'm doing I tell them I'm making a shopping list. Isabel demands that popsicles be put on the list. "For Felicity's throat," she adds piously, and Felicity wants Cocoa Puffs and olives. But after they see me dutifully write down these requests they decide to go in the family room and play at shooting aliens with laser guns. They can see me, anytime they like, engrossed in a task they approve of, and it doesn't appear to strike them as odd that I stand writing, for over an hour, what would have to be a very long grocery list.

By Friday they are as glad to get back to the Rye Street Montessori as I am to take them there. I watch them run up the walk and into the door, a winter wind turning their cheeks pink, and then I hurry home to telephone Victor, first at home and then at the farmhouse. He says to come out, of course. The only thing is that he has to be on campus at 11:00 for a meeting.

I debate as I drive; was there or wasn't there a slight hesitation in Victor's voice before he said *come?* Did he or did he not seem glad to hear my voice?

But there's nothing doubtful about the way he meets me in the kitchen doorway and gives me a hug that leaves me breathless. Through his shirt I can feel his ribs and his backbone; Victor's body always feels taut as though it might vibrate when touched.

"Did you miss me?"

"What do you think?"

"You did. You missed me. What are you going to do about it?"

"At this very minute I'm going to eat my breakfast. Then we'll see, won't we?"

Although I've eaten breakfast I'm suddenly hungry

too — through sheer relief, probably — and we both eat eggs and bacon and toast like farm hands.

"I did miss you, damn it," Victor says, eyeing me belligerently over the toast. "I felt deserted. And to top it off Kate telephoned and said she wasn't coming home for Thanksgiving. Prefers what will probably be a nearly empty dormitory to coming back and spending a couple of days with me."

"It doesn't mean she doesn't love you . . ."

"Oh, I know that. Annoys hell out of me, all the same."

Victor stabs two of the squares of toast at once and chews energetically. He's one of those people, I've noted before, who can't do only one thing at a time. While he chews he lines up more squares; he reaches over his shoulder, plucks two more pieces of bread from the toaster, offers them to me, and when I refuse he deftly spreads a sliver of butter over each. Whatever he does is to the point — he doesn't expend nervous energy in jumping up from the table to roam around but he's never still, either. So it isn't surprising that he has a list of publications two pages long and that he's chairman of the department and serving on several important committees. Nor does it surprise me, exactly, that he manages to fit me so neatly into the pattern of his days.

"You wouldn't believe it, would you," Victor says now, "but I hate living in an empty house. Without those little background noises of someone else moving around and breathing I start feeling self-conscious. Silence can be as loud as a thunderclap."

"You and Isabel and Felicity," I tell him. "They love background noise, too. Pity you can't provide it for each other." But seeing the look Victor is giving me I hasten to amend what I've said. "No, I'm not offering you the patter of small feet outside your door, Victor. Those are Walter's small feet . . . Walter's daughters' small feet . . ."

"I know perfectly well what you mean."

"Look, Victor," I say to him, taking his hand across the table, "we haven't seen each other for ten days, we're glad to be together again, and we don't have to ruin it by talking about things we know will upset us."

124

"You're right," he says, squeezing my hand. "Are you ready to come upstairs, woman?"

As Victor undresses he folds each piece of clothing and puts it on a chair all ready for a quick, efficient dressing later. I drop my clothes on the floor so I'm in bed before him, watching as he does the last thing—unhooking his watch strap and putting it, lying north to south, on his bedside table.

He comes into bed kicking his legs like someone treading water in order to warm up. "I don't want to come to you cold as a toad."

"You won't be cold long with me. You're already warming up, aren't you? Can't help it, can you?"

And Victor, laughing, holds me tightly to him and we roll, nipping each other's shoulders with our teeth.

It's the power we have over each other that we love and play on. What we like more than anything else is to keep the other just on the brink, hovering, panting, begging for release from a pleasure so great it is almost a torment. The line is fine, though, and sometimes we hang on a little too long and the climax comes before we're ready.

But this time we hold each other a long time in that delicious ecstasy and when we come—me first and then Victor—it takes us a long time to arouse from our dreams.

No matter how much we may want to keep the moment we slowly drift apart from a union that—for all its pleasures—is never, quite, the total and all encompassing one we thought it might be. Though it is always close, close.

As I come to lying by Victor's side and see his face again in whatever illumination the light provides—the lines momentarily smoothed at the corners of his mouth, the lids with their short black lashes unable to conceal the restlessness of those eyes that move as smoothly under the lids as though they are riding on oil—I feel the sadness of loss.

"What are you dreaming about, Victor?" I ask softly in his ear.

"Sunshine," he tells me instantly. "A woman in a wide

125

brimmed pink hat."

And then he opens his eyes suddenly, blinking at the light like someone who's just had a blindfold snatched away.

"Was it me? In the pink hat?"

"No, no, you'd look silly in a hat like that. Not you, not Olivia. Nobody I know. The Eternal Feminine, I suppose."

"What a romantic notion," I say, intrigued. "But I couldn't have a dream about the Eternal Masculine because I don't even know what he'd look like. Michelangelo's *David*, maybe? But no. I think I like a little more age and wisdom. When I try to come up with the Eternal Masculine all I can think of is you, or you maybe with a touch of Walter. I can't rise into the universal, or the myth, or whatever. And just look at all those women——the Virgin Mary and the Mona Lisa and Faust's Marguerite . . ."

But Victor, as I see very clearly by the studious way he's looking at the ceiling, is not listening. It's fine for *him* to lecture but heaven forbid that anyone should lecture to him.

Victor picks up his watch, looks at it, puts it down again, and stretches with his hands under his head. "Lee?" he says tentatively, but I push my face in the pillow and refuse to answer. If he won't let me talk then why should I let him? "Come on," he says, shaking my shoulder. "You aren't asleep, are you?"

"How could I be?" I say, flinging away from him to the far side of the bed.

"I've been thinking about Walter. Couldn't we talk about Walter for a few minutes?"

I don't answer but he goes ahead anyhow.

"I'd hate to tell you how many times I've seen Walter come into his office after class, put his briefcase on the right side of the desk, his jacket on a hook. Then before he can sit down he has to sharpen two pencils—— always two——and roll up his sleeves. Just like clockwork."

"So?" I say belligerently. "Look at you. Clothes folded, watch lying north to south . . ."

"Ah, but there's purpose in my order. I fold my clothes like that so I can dress in two minutes. But Walter uses his little rituals to make him feel safe. The unexpected, something he hasn't taken into account, drives him wild, doesn't it?"

"What if it does?"

"My point," Victor says, raising one finger imperiously in the air, "is that if you left Walter he wouldn't sink down into an abject heap as you seem to think he would. He'd be upset for awhile, I grant you that — he'd go into a tailspin, probably. But after he got used to the idea he wouldn't find it half bad. He'd have the girls three days a week, regular as clockwork, and he'd get used to not having you around. It's the pattern that's all important for Walter."

I have a vision of the girls trundling between Victor's house and Walter's, teddy bears under their arms, clean nighties in their FAO Swartz bags. They might even glory in having two households revolve around them; the girls would survive if anybody did. But what about poor Walter, saying hello to an empty house every afternoon, his voice lost in all that silence?

Just the thought brings tears to my eyes.

And yet . . . could it be possible? There is a picture in my mind of Walter standing over the stove making himself a perfect omelet, sliding it onto a pre-warmed plate and carrying it with an oven glove to the table where a folded napkin, the evening paper, and a plate of buttered bread with the crusts cut off are lying waiting for him.

He would sigh in a melancholy way and then unfold his newspaper, gently pick up the fork, and eat with good appetite . . .

"Oh, I just don't *know*," I say agitatedly. "I think you're probably all wrong about Walter but I just don't know . . . I can't bear to think of leaving him . . ."

"And me?"

I don't know that, either. Once Victor had us in the house, providing soothing background noises for his work, what then? Would he emerge only rarely from his study to ask for tea, to wonder, plaintively, if I've borrowed his black fountain pen, or have mislaid his paper clips?

127

"I don't want to give you up either," I tell him quickly. "Why can't I just keep you both?"

"You know this town and all those wagging tongues. It's only a matter of time, Lee. Face it."

"But I can't" I say, starting to cry.

Victor puts his arms around me but he doesn't offer any consolation. And, in fact, there is none he can give. What he says is only the truth.

12

Somehow I know — as though I had some kind of alarm clock ticking away inside my head, counting off the already allotted minutes — that I don't have much longer, and my lovemaking with Victor becomes more frantic. Now, as soon as I come in the door of the farmhouse I can't wait to get Victor upstairs to bed. He has to eat his toast on the way up the stairs, chewing a little desperately as I pull him along, ignoring the distress with which he looks back at his abandoned coffee and half eaten egg growing cold behind him on the table.

"I feel a little like a blob of Playdough some creative kid has gotten hold of," he says as I pull him along, but I know he likes it all the same. Like dancers who work well together, we egg each other on; we inspire in each other new heights of imagination and daring.

"Three times, just like that," Victor says, exhausted, lying with his arms flung across the bed. "You're insatiable, Lee. A demon. What are you trying to do, anyway? Use me all up? Drink me to the last drop?"

And it's true, through I'm trembling with exertion and my skin is tender from being rubbed against Victor's hairy chest, that I'm already eyeing wistfully Victor's prick which is lying in flaccid repose against his thigh. Already I want it again; to keep it for awhile longer. My stamina is greater than his and it isn't just the difference in our ages, either.

I know that the clock is ticking away and not even I know what position the hands must reach to set off the alarm, or how close they are to that position.

At the moments of greatest pleasure while we lie on our sides, fully enjoined, just beginning to thrust slowly, I suddenly freeze and whisper, "What was that? Did you hear a car in the driveway?"

And we listen, uncertain, until, cursing, Victor runs across the floor, crouched from the cold, and looks out the window to assure me that Walter hasn't arrived in the driveway in somebody's borrowed car to catch us in the act.

I expect danger and discovery—from Shirley Wilson or some other busybody, to intercept and interpret correctly some glance that may flash between Victor and me at a party. What I do not expect is that danger should slip in unnoticed in a way I hadn't thought about.

But, of course, the very closeness that Walter and I have always shared makes me vulnerable. Haven't I said that we can often read each other's thoughts? There is no defense that I know of that I can use against his intuition.

There is a night when I suddenly open my eyes, escaping a bad dream, and see light and a face directly above my own.

"It's only me," Walter says so hastily that I know I must have cried out.

He has been watching me, I feel, not just looking, and in the back of his eyes I can see uncertainty, maybe a question.

"What are you doing that for, staring at me in the middle of the night?" I say indignantly, scrambling to sit up, holding for some reason my thin pillow over my chest as though I expected him to hit me.

Walter leans back against his pillows and I see that he looks tired; they're lines of strain around his eyes, masking the old guilelessness. "I didn't mean to scare you. Only I'd just had a bad dream and wanted to make sure I was awake. You were having a bad dream, too, weren't you? At least your eyes were darting under your lids . . ."

I look at Walter's face but can't tell anything; that guilelessness could be a shield for anything. My own face, I'm sure, is much more furtive.

"I was in this tunnel and some man was chasing me with a gun . . ."

"Really?" Walter says, sliding down in the bed, propping himself on one elbow. "Do you remember anything else?"

As soon as he asks I know who the man was and why I had reason to fear him, but I'm not going to tell Walter that *he* was that sinister figure, following me, knowing always which turning I was going to take.

"Oh, it's a very common dream isn't it? Being chased that way?"

Walter shakes his head doubtfully as though to say *perhaps*.

"I must have told you this before, haven't I? About the way Dad kept a pistol in his bedside table?"

"On our wedding night, Walter, in between bouts of throwing up . . ."

"Of course he said it was for burglars . . ."

"And you knew it was for Nina's lovers. I know, Walter. I've heard the story."

My hand trembling only slightly, I pick up a book from the floor and hold it in front of my face. Walter, though, doesn't shift position.

"I sometimes wonder what would have happened if he'd come home sometime from tramping Canadian bogs after elk and found Mother in bed with some man. I actually think he'd probably have just stood there, too overcome with glee to do anything. I mean, think how it must have been for him to *expect* something like that, to be sure that somewhere, somehow, the scene was taking place even though, stalk as he would, he could never glimpse anything. And then, right there in broad daylight, was the very thing he'd searched for so long. Don't you think that the sight might have relieved him in some strange way?"

"No. I think he'd have gone into a terrible rage, taken that pistol out of his drawer, and shot them both before he even thought."

"Do you?" Walter says, his eyes studying my face. "I wonder . . ." but of course he did have a terrible temper."

Walter reaches under the bed for his slippers and puts on his dressing gown — one of deep red silk that had belonged to Leon before he died. When Nina tried to give Walter some of Leon's clothes Walter had first refused, but I'd talked him into taking a few things. Leon and Walter were the same size and Leon's clothes were much better than we could afford on an academic salary. I couldn't bear the waste.

"I'm going down to make some Ovaltine. Coming?"

I tell him that I'll be down in a few minutes and Walter goes off down the stairs, the heels of his slippers slapping on the treads.

As soon as he's gone I climb across the bed and furtively open the drawer of his bedside table. I have to feel all through it before I'm convinced that Leon's old pistol isn't lying there under class notes for Art of the Western World. But of course that's not the only possible hiding place; he could have put it somewhere else a lot less obvious than his bedside table. So I rummage through shoe boxes in the back of the closet and run my hands through his shirt drawer. Nothing.

In the middle of a search behind his books in the bookcase I'm suddenly struck by a new thought which sends me running to my own bedside table. Perhaps it was the search for something hidden that made me suddenly aware of the vulnerability of my own secrets. In any case, I feverishly paw through the rubble of old concert programs, letters, note cards scribbled with ideas for stories in the bottom drawer of my nightstand. At the bottom of the heap I lift out Felicity's baby book, but under that there is nothing, only the bare wood which I rub my fingers over frantically. I dump everything on the bed and rake through it. But there is no doubt. Olivia's black book is no longer in my drawer.

I can't understand it. I *must* have put the book somewhere else. And yet I know I haven't. That is the only place I have ever put it in the house. But if this is so, if—as I think—Walter has found the black book and taken it from my drawer, what does this mean? Why would he do a thing like that?

I ponder this question as I go down the stairs, but I can come to no conclusion. All I know is that secrets breed more secrets, that something dangerous has entered our marriage that wasn't there before.

When I come downstairs, Walter is leaning over the stove beating the hot milk with a whisk, and it is such a moment of domestic tranquility that I can't believe that anything dangerous

132

lies below the surface. Yet isn't it strange that Walter doesn't even bother to look around when I come in? Isn't there something self-conscious about the way he's leaning there, his eyes fixed on the milk?

"The milk's just about to boil . . ."

Walter sets my mug in front of me at the table and pours in the hot milk without spilling even a drop, his precision almost uncanny. But with me it's different. Anxiety makes my eyes glaze so I stare fixedly at one spot until my eyes feel dry.

"What's wrong?" Walter says. "Do I have Ovaltine on my chin? You have such a funny look on your face."

No, no Ovaltine, I assure him.

For the first time in our five years of marriage I look up at Walter's face and see it, for one terrible moment, as the face of a stranger, as mysterious to me as one of those squat figures the Mayans made out of stone.

The next morning, as soon as I am alone in the house, I try to reach Victor by telephone. But it's not until 1:30 that I finally reach him and then he's rushing off to a committee meeting.

I tell him I have to see him.

"What? Now? I can't, Lee. I've got this meeting and then a student . . ."

I tell him I have to see him that afternoon.

"Is it urgent? Because, look, Lee . . ."

I tell him it's urgent. When and where can I see him?

That, it becomes evident, is a difficult problem. Not at my house, of course, and not at his. Office on campus too risky. Farmhouse impossible in the afternoons. "Maybe the IGA in front of the flour and sugar?" I say desperately. But Victor has another idea.

"Swimming pool at the gym. It's faculty swim from 3:30 to 5:30, and I'll see you there at quarter to four."

So at quarter to four, having left Faith to babysit the girls for an hour, I walk self-consciously into the steamy, womby warmth of the room that houses the indoor swimming pool. I hate the slimy feel of the wet concrete under my feet and I hate to be in a room as crowded with humanity as some painting of the Last Judgment.

And I hate most of all the fact that Victor isn't here yet and I must fool around waiting for him, doing my careful and measured crawl up and down between the bodies.

By the time he does show up I am already shivering under my towel, but he has to go and take that showy dive from the next to the highest board, cutting into the water like a knife through soft butter.

Yet I have to admit that he is right to make that dive, to swim up and down before he finally joins me in what must appear to be an unpremeditated meeting on the bench. While Victor stands in front of me vigorously rubbing with his towel, not an eye is turned in our direction and when he sits he leaves at least a foot of space between us.

"Don't we look like we're sitting here talking about the weather?" he says out of the corner of his mouth. "Just remember not to look in my direction too much, all right?"

"Victor," I say, keeping my gaze on two boys who are falling backwards into the water with their hands over their noses, "I think Walter knows about us."

"How come?"

"Because he was bound to, I guess."

"But what makes you think so?"

"You remember Olivia's black book? Well, I had it in my bedside table under a lot of other things and now it's gone."

Victor gives me a bewildered look. "I don't understand what you're saying."

"It was there and now it's gone. Walter's taken it."

"You've just misplaced it."

"I haven't. That was the only place I ever put it."

"But why would he want it?"

"I don't know why he wants it. Evidence I suppose."

"But evidence of what, Lee? It doesn't make any sense."

"Evidence that something's wrong. I don't know. But I can tell from the way he looks at me he knows something."

Victor starts shaking his head and I know exactly what he's thinking.

"It's not just my imagination, Victor. I *know* Walter. And I can tell you that he's started looking at me in a way I don't like."

"I think it's only your guilty conscience."

"Look! I didn't even *have* a guilty conscience until he began giving me this odd look."

"Of course you've got a guilty conscience. You're not the sort of person who goes around having affairs all the time. It's only natural to have a guilty conscience . . ."

"All I want to know is what I should do now!"

I'm getting agitated, my voice is rising, and Victor raises his hand as a warning signal.

"Lee, I doubt very much that Walter knows. And even if he does, what *can* you do?"

"Maybe I shouldn't see you so often . . ."

"Why don't we talk about it tomorrow? Will you come out to the farmhouse, same as always?"

I say yes, I'll come, and I do, arriving at the farmhouse at my usual time, but we don't do much talking.

Like Paolo and Olivia, we leave a trail of clothes to the bed; our lovemaking has never been so good or so frenzied. We have gone beyond the black book and are charting waters of our own.

13

It's the 17th of December, a Wednesday, and it's snowing in that kind of fitful, constipated way that gets on everybody's nerves. When I burst in the door of the farmhouse, stamping off snow, dropping gloves, unwinding my scarf, Victor takes one look and starts chewing hard and grabbing for another piece of toast. "You can eat anytime," I tell him, grabbing his arm and stopping it halfway to his coffee cup. "You'll like what I thought up in the bath last night."

"Can't it wait five minutes? Just until I eat this piece of toast and have another few swallows of coffee? I'm no good without coffee in the mornings and I'll have more staying power if you let me finish my breakfast."

"Why didn't you get up earlier then? You know what time I get here. And we don't have much time . . ."

So we rush up stairs as though we're being chased, Victor losing a slipper on the way and me starting on my shirt buttons. We're so excited by the time we get in bed that there isn't any time for the variation I've thought up. Like someone giving birth in a taxi, we have no time for embellishments.

"You're going to kill me," Victor groans. "Hardly any breakfast and I know this is just a lull between storms."

"Yep."

"Look! Have a little consideration, will you? I've got gray in my hair. I'm old enough to be your father . . ."

"Maybe I'll let you have your breakfast later, if you're good."

"Oh, you'll be sorry. You'll wish you'd let sleeping dogs lie . . ."

"Ah, but it's not lying at all. Out of the ashes, there it comes . . ."

136

We don't even hear the car until, just under the window, the motor races and then dies.

We freeze where we are, our blood going cold. "Walter!" I say, too terrified to move. It's Victor who leaps up and runs to the window, crouching so his head won't show above the sill. When he peeks through the glass, though, he grabs the sill and looks wildly around the room. "Oh my god! It's Kate!"

"Kate?" I say stupidly. "Who's Kate?"

"Kate, Kate, my daughter Kate!" Victor says, springing for his clothes and putting on shirt and trousers more rapidly than I've ever seen anybody dress. "She wasn't meant to get here before Friday."

We bump into each other as I pull on my jeans and reach for my sweater.

"I think you should stay up here," he says. "Or, no, no you can't do that! She'll have seen your car. We'd better go down together. I'll explain about your writing."

"In your bedroom? Why should I be writing in your bedroom?"

"Maybe we can get downstairs . . ."

But that, of course, is impossible. Even as he speaks the car door slams, and from the parking place under the walnut trees it's only ten feet to the house.

We cram our feet into shoes, but when we hear the fateful rattle on the door we are only to the top of the stairs and in Victor's house that means that our goose is cooked. The stairs are in plain view from the back door so we have no choice but to descend them as Kate watches.

She has already swung open the door and called out "Hi" before she sees us coming down the stairs, Victor in front, our lips stretched into what must be strange smiles.

"Darling!" Victor says, spreading his arms wide; they come together at the bottom of the stairs for an embrace that looks fervent enough. But I suspect that I'm the one already cast in the heavy role. That as far as Kate is concerned this rather squalid homecoming is probably my fault and that Victor is only an

137

innocent victim.

The two of them are blocking the foot of the stairs and I have to wait on the third step, until Victor moves aside and allows me to descend.

"Oh, and of course you know Lee," Victor says, which is stupid since I've known Kate since she was fifteen.

He's standing with his arm around Kate's shoulders, and I feel the outsider, no mistake about that.

"Lee uses the house here as a studio in the mornings. As a place to write. We were just taking a look at a leak in one of the bedroom ceilings."

"Do you know a lot about leaks in ceilings?" Kate asks, giving me an innocent look.

"Not too much . . ."

"She was just commiserating with me," Victor says, giving me a look I can only describe as fishy. "I'm afraid I interrupted her in the middle of some piece of deathless prose."

He smiles a wide, false smile, and I'm suddenly furious with him. I know very well what that "deathless prose" crack is meant to convey. It's a way of reducing my importance, of showing Kate that I am no more than a casual figure around here. Prose that is really deathless is never described that way, not even by some half-assed academic.

"Well, I'll just leave you two alone," I say, giving Victor a dirty look. My feelings are hurt and I feel betrayed. "I couldn't get anymore done on my deathless prose as you call it this morning anyway." When I look at him, Victor rolls his eyes heavenward to show, I suppose, that everything has gotten out of control and I shouldn't blame him too harshly for playing the clown. But I do.

My jacket is still lying collapsed sideways by the door as though it contained the invisible body of somebody who'd gotten himself shot, and my gloves are lying, five feet apart, marking a kind of path between table and stairs. I pick them up as nonchalantly as I can, put on my jacket, and depart.

I am angry with Victor—really fed up. And where did he come up with that stupid leak in the ceiling business? A leak in the ceiling could be a *metaphor* for sex, for heaven's sake. I can just see someone winking lewdly and saying, "Come on upstairs and let's see if we can't fix that leak of yours." But maybe Freud was right after all and we can't even open our mouths without giving ourselves away. That what we most want to avoid saying comes out in veiled form anyway. We won't rest until we've given ourselves away, betrayed ourselves, made ourselves look like fools. That in some diabolical way we are bound to do these things.

Though why I should want Kate to know her father and her mother's best friend should have spent the morning in bed fixing each other's leaking ceilings is more than I know. Still, there I stood on the stairs, with that silly smile on my face, the very picture of guilt.

I don't even know Kate, for heaven's sake, although she was around a lot on those afternoons I came over to visit Olivia. She was in the background somewhere, sulking, listening to the Rolling Stones or somebody, making Olivia suffer through her adolescent miseries with her. But she was always close to Victor; he was the one she obviously loved. She never showed much interest in Olivia's friends and I didn't go exactly out of my way to talk to her.

But now she's a college girl, in her third year at Swarthmore, and could be, and probably is, greatly changed.

That afternoon I answer the telephone to hear Victor whispering on the other end.

"Yes, of course it's me, and why are you whispering?"

"Was I?" he says, turning on his voice. "I'm sorry. I'm in my office."

"Is Kate there with you?"

"No, no, I'm alone." There's a silence during which Victor clears his throat. "I'm afraid that as long as Kate is here we can't get together, Lee."

"Don't you think I realize that?"

"It isn't my fault, you know. I didn't expect her in . . ."

"Who's blaming you?"

"You sound a little angry to me. Or am I mistaken?"

"You're not mistaken but that's not the reason."

"I know I didn't handle this morning very well but it was awkward . . ."

Another silence falls over the wire. I'm not going to let him off easily.

"Oh, there is one thing, Lee. Kate said she'd like to get together with you. Tomorrow, maybe, if you're free."

I'm taken aback and can't hide my surprise. "With me? Why?"

"I think she always liked you. She's known you for years . . ."

That doesn't explain why Kate would want to talk to me, but I see no way out of it. I tell Victor I'll drive out in the morning after I take the girls to nursery school.

"And I'll be seeing you Saturday night, won't I? At the Stacks?"

I tell him that I suppose he will unless I can think of a way to get out of the Stacks' annual Christmas party.

The next day the sky is covered with thick, gray cloud and it is raining and sleeting at the same time. Or, at least there is rain in the air; as soon as it lands on something—a tree limb or the windshield of a car—it turns to ice. The defrost has never been any good in our Toyota and the frail stream of warm air sliding up the windshield is no match for the ice which locks the wiper into an ever decreasing triangle. Soon I have to lean over the wheel and peer out a tiny space one inch by one inch, my nose practically pressing against the glass. Walter would have a fit if he knew I was driving like that but it's his fault we have the Toyota anyway; like a lot of academics he distrusts American junk, but that only means that we're easy targets for foreign junk. Walter's colleagues have Volvos which won't start in the rain, or they have Volkswagons in which they freeze, or Toyotas they can't see out of five months of the year.

I consider turning back halfway to the farmhouse, but I can't see well enough to turn back, either. So I push on and arrive, at last, at the turning under the trees.

There is a thin, wavery stream of smoke coming from the chimney so I assume that Kate is in the house somewhere though I have to wait at the door after I knock with the icy rain falling on my face.

"Oh, sorry," Kate says as she opens the door. "I was just in the middle of putting more wood on the fire and I had to put the screen back."

She thrusts her hand in my direction and I shake it; I suppose that this is one of those gestures of solidarity that women make together these days.

Kate seems to have grown since she was a high school girl; at least she's put on weight and her face which used to be small and heartshaped appears to have grown broader too. Or perhaps it only looks broader because she's wearing her hair pulled back; at the corners of her mouth there are a few fine, bronze colored hairs which remind me, with a little shock, that she's no longer just a girl.

We take chairs opposite each other, on either side of the fireplace and we sit like that for a silence that goes on a little too long for comfort before Kate asks, with an abruptness that startles me, "You and Dad are lovers, aren't you?"

"Well, I don't suppose there's any point denying it . . ."

"I'm afraid I must have looked surprised when I saw you coming down the stairs . . ."

"Not as surprised as we were to see you," I tell her, trying to make a feeble joke which she ignores. Olivia, come to think of it, never had a sense of humor, either.

"Sorry about that. Of course I know Dad's here alone, now, a man in his prime and I'm just glad he's found somebody. You know that Mother is terribly happy with Paolo."

"Seems so."

Kate leans forward and looks at me with the same kind of intensity that Victor often shows. "It made me so *sad*, Lee, to see two grown people looking so guilty about something so beautiful. I just wanted you to know that I'm glad for the two of you, I really am."

"That's very nice," I say, a little primly. I'm only ten years older than Kate but the difference might as well be fifty. I feel suddenly I'm already archaic.

"You see I *understand* it all so perfectly. I mean, if it weren't for David . . . and Linda . . . I might have gotten upset. I just wouldn't have understood. But as it is I *do*. I know just how it is."

Kate looks at me with expectant eyes.

"Who's David?" I see that this is the question I'm supposed to ask.

"Oh, I'm sorry! I thought you could tell. David's my lover. An older man, oh, about Dad's age, as it happens. A wonderful man, really. And Linda's wonderful too. Just extraordinary . . ."

"Linda?"

"David's wife. And a very good friend of mine."

"You mean she knows? About you and David?"

I imagine Linda, some paraplegic in a wheelchair saying sweetly, 'Now, you two just run along and enjoy yourselves. Remember that if you're happy I'm happy.' "

"Of course she knows. I told David from the very beginning that I wouldn't build my happiness on someone else's unhappiness. I just wouldn't leave Linda out. David kept saying, 'But we can't tell Linda. She just couldn't take it.' But I knew better and I insisted. Either we all got together and talked the thing over, discussing it until a consensus was reached, or I'd end it right there."

"And did you? All get together?"

"Sure. Oh, it was a little bit hard in the beginning. We're so used to thinking possessively about each other. It took Linda awhile to see that I just wanted to share David, not to take him away from her. How could I? He's not some apple that we can hand back and forth. I mean, neither of us *owns* him. It took awhile but now Linda and I are friends too. It's just beautiful, what's happened."

I don't know if Kate is crazy, or if, maybe, she really has reached some higher plane of living than I would have thought possible. I wonder if it could happen — if it even lies in the realm of possibility — that I could become the apple passed back and forth between Walter and Victor, but I just can't believe it. Maybe I'm already too old, or something, to grasp what Kate is saying, but jealousy just doesn't seem to me so easily overcome.

"To me all that sounds a little bizarre . . ."

"No, no, but it isn't," Kate says, giving me that intense gaze

142

of someone who has found the Light. "Sneaking around and lying are bizarre, but what's bizarre about honesty? Lies hurt everybody."

"But don't you think honesty can be even worse?"

"If I did I wouldn't be telling you all this. Don't you think Linda would have known, really, that something was up with David, anyhow, and have felt miserable and lonely? Isn't it much better to be included?"

"But if you and David are in bed together and Linda's not with you she's still excluded, isn't she?"

"I'm excluded, too, when David and Linda . . . But that's not the point."

I can see that Kate's face is growing a little stiff with patience; obviously I'm a difficult pupil, the kind who never seems to understand what's being said.

"All I want," Kate says earnestly, "is for Dad — and you — to be happy. And I think you're making life difficult for yourselves. All that guilt. And it doesn't have to be that way."

This is where I came in, more or less.

"What works for you I just don't think would work for us, though I certainly do appreciate you're telling me about David and Linda and you . . ."

"Sometimes you need a little boost in the beginning. It's hard to take that first step. To leading an open, honest life, I mean."

"Oh, I'm sure it is. Very very difficult. As far as I'm concerned nearly impossible . . ."

"But I'm sure you'll do the right thing, you know. Wouldn't it be wonderful if Mother and Paolo and you and Dad and your husband could all be together living honest, direct lives without any of the garbage about jealousy and possessiveness and that whole bad scene . . ."

"Oh sure, sure," I say as I stand up to leave. "But that's a whole new world, probably, as far as I can see . . ."

Kate smiles encouragingly, as someone who has the secret.

At the door we embrace and Kate gives me a hearty, bracing sqeeze. She has done her duty; she has tried to put my feet on the right path and she seems to believe, by the way that she's looking at

143

me, that I, too, will see the Light and act accordingly.

Nothing on earth, though, would make me arrange the confrontation that Kate seems to think so necessary to the happiness of all the people involved. Linda may be either extraordinary or merely masochistic — I don't know anything about Linda — but I do know something about Walter.

14

The trip back to town is perilous. There is hardly any traffic on the highway but when I do see another car in the distance, approaching with the same desperate caution with which I'm approaching *it*, I start making anxious moaning sounds. The worst moment is when we're only feet apart and I'm afraid that the very intensity of my desire to pass without wavering will draw me like a nail sliding onto the end of a magnet directly into the path of the other car. So I look straight ahead as though I'm wearing blinkers, seeing only through a narrow band through the ice that coats the windshield—a narrow band that allows me to see only what I must.

When I reach the Rye Street Montessori and shuffle up the walk, fearful of letting my boots lose contact with the earth even for a moment, I see that Isabel and Felicity are already waiting for me behind the glass door.

"Everyone else's mommies came for them ages ago," Isabel says accusingly when I reach them.

"I sent the children home early," Mrs. Faraday says, "only I wasn't able to reach you. They've started to close some of the roads."

"I was just on one that should have been closed," I tell her as I take the girls' hands.

Isabel and Felicity, since they're so near the ground anyway, have no fear of falling on the ice. They like it, in fact, and scoot their boots in order to slide. I feel I'm imperiled between them but they don't want to let go my hands and though I know I'm far less a stabilizing force than they realize, I'm touched by their confidence in me and allow them to hang on until we reach the car.

By the time Walter comes home at 3:30, much earlier than usual, it seems to me likely that we're all going to be entombed in ice like those wooly mammoths dug up after thousands of years with the flowers they'd eaten for their last meal still only partly digested in their stomachs.

There is a thick layer of ice around every tree limb and the poor bushes are weighed down to the ground, their flimsy branches spayed around them like the legs of stepped on spiders. When I let Patsy outside to pee he comes back in a few minutes with ice already crusting on his fur.

"How much weight can the trees take?" I ask Walter. "And what about the roof? It's an old house, after all, and perhaps everything is weakened by age."

I can imagine the whole thing caving in, the rafters and trusses and braces all giving way at once with a terrible splintering noise entombing us under the rubble.

But Walter, who worries so much about trifles, is strangely calm, even happy, in a house encased in ice. He leads us from window to window making pleased whistlings through his teeth. Ice coats the glass, too, so that objects blur and cannot be distinguished one from the other. The whole world outside our house seems to have melted or fused. Only from the south windows, which are protected by an overhanging roof, can we see out.

And this is what Walter most loves. To have his family together around him and protected from the dangers of the world that lie outside our windows. No thieves or murderers or arsonists will be out on a night like this and even if we wanted to we cannot leave our shelter. We are as some prehistoric family, huddled together for warmth and safety in the back of our cave.

We eat in front of the fire, listening to the tinkle of ice on ice as some overburdened twig falls to the ground or to the groaning as the wind stirs one of the heavily coated tree limbs. The girls are directly in front of the fire, Walter and I sitting behind on the rug, our shoulders and thighs brushing together. Everything which lies beyond our windows fades, blurs, ceases to have existence.

"We're bears in our houses," Isabel says, pushing her plate out of the way and lying curled up on the rug, her feet and hands reaching toward the fire. "We've just gotten up to eat our dinners and then we're going back to bed."

146

"If we were really bears we'd just sleep all winter," I tell her. "We wouldn't even know anything unless maybe we were having a dream."

"They just don't go *outside* all winter," Isabel says in a sleepy voice. "They sleep a lot but they still have to get up to eat and feed their babies."

Felicity curls up with Isabel so they're both looking into the fire, their heads touching. Their hair is nearly the same color, Felicity's only a little lighter than Isabel's — brown with a good deal of red that catches the firelight.

Almost immediately Felicity goes to sleep with her thumb lying in the corner of her mouth. Every once in awhile she knows it's there, and sucks on it until her lips part again and she moves into a deeper level of sleep. Isabel's eyelids keep sliding over her eyes though she wants to stay awake. She battles against her sleepiness but can't win.

"Aren't they sweet?" Walter whispers in my ear, and of course they are. It's curious what a perfect blend of the two of us they are—how Felicity has Walter's round face but my mouth and Isabel has my thin face and Walter's small, blunt nose. Walter and I will always be bound together in our children's faces.

Walter reaches out his hand for mine and I lay my hand in his palm. With his finger he traces the lines — of heart, mind and longevity.

"Are you happy?" he asks, still looking at my hand.

I say with some surprise that I am.

He, too, is happy. He thinks that from now on he won't be so moody.

"I thought I was the moody one."

"You too. Your thoughts have seemed a long way away . . ."

"Not tonight. My thoughts are right here tonight."

Walter nods. He knows that. Of course he can read my moods if not my thoughts.

It's odd, but as I sit here in front of the fire with Walter I feel that Victor has blurred a little, slid into the background as has everything else which lies beyond our blanked out windows. He and Kate are iced inside their own house and if I were there with them I wouldn't be happy.

No, I have a fantasy. At this very moment as we are all together in this peaceful way, suddenly, instantaneously, we are sealed tight in ice, not to be dug up until 2,000 years from now. Intact, every hair preserved. Through the glass in the museum where we are preserved in our zero temperature room, the visitors peer and exclaim.

Imperiously a guide taps our glass to get silence. "And here you have a North American family, ladies and gentlemen, who lived in the 1970's. Note the perfect detail. You can see every hair on the little girls' heads. (Oooooo, ahhhhh, look at that!) And note that the man and woman are holding hands. It even looks as though they may have been smiling at that last, climatic moment. Yes? Was there a question? Did they know they were being frozen? As far as scientists can make out this ice age did fall very rapidly, almost instantaneously, so perhaps they had no warning at all. Or perhaps they did and they chose to die together that way, in the family unit which was the way people usually lived in those days. (Isn't that quaint, though!) You ask if they had names? Well, remember this was 2,000 years ago and so whatever we say about them is a guess. But we do refer to them officially as the Smith family, since that was a typical name of the period. I do recollect, though, that there used to be an old fellow who worked her a lot, a paleontologist, who used to refer to them as Adam and Eve, but I can't explain the significance of those names, if there is one. He was a pretty queer old fellow."

Later on, after we have carried the girls upstairs, slipped them in their beds and patted the blankets around their chins, Walter and I lie together in the middle of our bed and listen to the ice creak with a sound like breaking bones. We put our arms around each other and our knees interlace like someone sliding the fingers of one hand between the knuckles of the other.

"Lee," Walter says in my ear. "I have something to confess to you. Oh, I feel silly saying this. But I've taken something of yours."

"As long as it's not my toothbrush . . ."

"No, no, it's a book. Oh, this is bad, really. I'm embarrassed. But I was looking for your address book one night and I came across this black book — the writing wasn't yours, or I really wouldn't have read it . . ."

"Olivia's book!"

"Yes, of course, Olivia. I finally figured it out. The handwriting. Rome. Once I started reading it I had to go on, awful as it was. The writing is terrible, isn't it? But it does have a certain fascination . . ."

"Oh I know, I know. Do you think Olivia would be horrified or pleased to think we'd read it?"

"First horrified, then pleased."

Walter hesitates and I know he's pondering something important.

"I thought, perhaps, you know, that you might want to try out some of the things she writes about. I know I'm not very imaginative about trying new things. I'm such a stick in the mud."

I am ridiculously relieved to find that my paranoia over the black book was unjustified. Where I had feared traps and Leon's old pistol, Walter had only been innocently trying to improve our marriage. So perhaps I'd been wrong about other things as well and Walter had never, even for a moment, felt any suspiciousness about me.

The possibility that I was going to be allowed to get away with something, to get by scot free with Victor and all the rest, so fills me with euphoria that when Walter asks shyly if I want to try something out of the black book I say why not?

It's our best lovemaking for a long time.

"Shall I tell you something?" Walter says when we're lying near sleep. "One day when I was lying on Fassbinder's couch I realized something very odd. I'd always had this feeling, when we made love, that my father was sort of floating above our heads, watching from the corner over there. Up by the ceiling with his legs crossed, rubbing his fingernails on his lapel, sort of sneering at the performance."

"Was he up there this time, do you think?"

"He was hanging around, back there in the shadows, but this

149

time I felt he was on my side. Instead of sneering he was saying things like 'Not bad. Good job, boy.' "

Maybe Walter has sneaked from Leon what he needed as I've sneaked what I needed from Victor and we are both making off with our prizes like dogs with bones. Nor does the symbolism of that simile escape me.

15

On Saturday morning — the day of the Stacks' party — I open my eyes to snow falling thickly from a white sky, and to Walter's singing from the kitchen. In a kind of croaking bass comes the strains of "Maybe, Baby." This is one of the few songs Walter knows and he only sings it when he's especially happy.

"May — be, ba — by, you were meant for meee . . . may — be, ba-by, this was meant to bee . . . and may-be, ba-by, we'll get to — geth — er a — gain."

It's clear that Walter is making breakfast and I conclude from certain bangings and clangings I can hear that the girls are helping him with his labors.

Eventually the noise ascends the stairs and Walter, with the girls in front, comes into the bedroom bearing a breakfast tray.

"It's snowing!" the girls say, jumping on the bed. "It's snowing, it's pouring, the old man's roaring!"

"That's not how it goes," I tell them, but they don't care. By the looks of the sky it will be the first big snow of the year.

Walter has brought toast, butter, strawberry jam, a pot of coffee, and a jug of milk and he makes the girls settle down, one on each side of me, before he'll give them anything to eat. He sits crosslegged in front of us, and though we spill crumbs in the sheets and the girls smear jam on the pillowcases it doesn't matter since Saturday is sheet changing day anyway.

For two days Walter has been in a very good mood and he's obviously in an especially happy one this morning. A storm has passed over our heads, and here we are, all together and safe.

What seemed to me so intolerable not long ago no longer seems so difficult. We take what we need — the way Victor once put the Baptistry doors in his head for good. He would never see them again as he had in that first, revelatory moment, but, on the

151

other hand, he wouldn't have to since afterwards they had become a part of his very brain cells.

Walter decides that it's a cooking day and spends the morning making chicken pilaf. Walter likes to feed us, to nurture us — he likes this role more than I do.

"Know what I'd like to do this afternoon?" he says, giving me a lewd wink across the table.

"You've got a hope," I tell him, looking meaningfully at the girls.

"How about a nice cozy nap this afternoon?" Walter says to them, looking hopeful. They don't bother to answer; the question is obviously a silly one.

"I'll even read you that coy English book that you're so fond of. The one about little Grey Rabbit. What's nicer than reading in a warm, soft bed on a snowy afternoon?"

The girls are not unwilling to be read to; they're just unwilling to sleep. I know very well what will happen, but while Walter is gamefully reading, I go outside to make a half-hearted attempt to clear the driveway. Since it's still snowing my efforts can't amount to much, but I like to be outside, to be in the storm instead of watching it from behind glass. The air is still and though full of snow is not very cold. It's pleasant out there bending and scooping snow in my shovel and throwing it into a heap beside the drive.

I seem to be the only person stirring, but to my surprise I see the dim figure of the mailman coming down what would ordinarily be the walk. He looks like a ghostly apparition and I think for a moment that perhaps he *is* — that he's the ghost of some earlier, dutiful mailman who believed in the motto of the U.S. Mail: neither wind nor snow nor dark of night shall keep the postman from his appointed rounds. But, no, it actually is Mr. Sleigleman with a few soggy pieces of mail which he hands to me before he trudges on into the swirling white.

A postcard from Nina of brilliantly blue sky and water and a few artfully placed cyprus trees, a bill from the oil company, and a letter to Walter from a student. This is the time of year, around Christmas, when any job openings in art history should be apparent, that former students remember their old teachers.

152

I stick everything in the pocket of my jacket and go on flinging shovelfuls of snow onto the bank until Walter sticks his head out the door and says, which is no surprise, that he can't get the girls to go to sleep.

"Of course you can't," I tell him as I prop my shovel against the doorjam and go on inside. "They aren't dummies. They never do anything you especially want them to. If you wanted them to stay awake for some reason they'd go to sleep instantly."

"Well, we won't stay too late at the party," Walter says, looking hopeful again. "And tomorrow's Sunday and we can sleep late."

When Faith Krause arrives at 8:00, to babysit, the girls are in their gowns but are still very much awake. They are leaping back and forth between their beds flapping their arms, since Isabel has decreed that they should play Peter Pan flying off to the Island of Forgotten Boys. She, of course, is Peter and Felicity is assigned the role of Wendy although what she wants to be is Tinker Bell. "You can't be Tinker Bell because we can pretend Tinker Bell," Isabel says with the kind of cutting logic that always throws Felicity into despair. "You have to be Wendy, Patsy has to be the crocodile, and Faith can be Captain Hook."

Felicity retreats in tears under a pillow until Faith, who is used to crises of this sort in her own house, pulls her out and wipes off her cheeks with her shirttail. "Felicity can be Wendy *and* Tinker Bell. Otherwise we'll have to play something else."

"Okay," Isabel says without any more ado, and begins taking off for flight again.

"Why can't *we* do that with the girls?" I ask Walter as I go to our bedroom and shut the door. "They always listen more to Faith than they do to us."

"The power of novelty, probably. Or maybe Faith would have real talent as a lion tamer."

Walter goes off to take a bath and I open my closet door and look unhappily at the clothes hanging inside.

"Hey, Faith!" I call down the hallway. "What's your mother wearing to the party?"

"Nothing special. A maternity smock."

153

Of course. One of the reasons to get pregnant again.

But it doesn't make any difference what I wear, not to this party, anyway. Who's going to dress up to trudge three or four blocks through a snowstorm? I put on my good black slacks and a sweater and consider the thing done. Walter, though, is going to be a lot pokier. Walter will certainly wear a shirt and tie since he's a little stuffy about things like that.

While I'm waiting, I remember Nina's card that came in the mail and which I haven't even read yet. So I go downstairs and take the card and the letter to Walter from my jacket pocket. The oil bill can stay where it is. I don't even want to know what the oil bill is.

I put Walter's letter beside his lamp and lie down on the bed to read Nina's card.

Dears: I came over here to Sicily on the 10th, but it's not what I expected. Nothing but rain, rain, rain until I think even my head is probably getting soggy, like a cabbage left outside to freeze. I'm homesick for good, clean American snow. What do you think? Should I give it a try?

When Walter comes out of the bathroom I tell him that Nina is thinking of coming home.

Walter skims the card and starts getting excited. "Do you think, maybe, by Christmas? If we telephoned? But all the flights just before Christmas may be booked."

"I wouldn't have thought there were that many stray Americans in Europe trying to get home for Christmas."

Walter puts his arms into his shirt. "Okay. We'll telephone tomorrow during the cheap rates."

"I'll get curtains for the spare bedroom, though knowing Nina, she wouldn't notice anyway." I pick up his letter from the beside table and show it to him. "From a student I think."

Walter pulls on grey flannel trousers and sits on the edge of the bed to put on his socks. He picks up the letter from under the lamp and starts absently running his finger under the envelope flap.

"How long do you think she'll stay? It wouldn't surprise me a bit if she stayed three days and suddenly got an overwhelming urge to go off to the Canary Islands. But, on the other hand, maybe she is tired of gallivanting and will stay until spring. She's one of the few people alive I would really like to have stay . . ."

"I know," Walter says absently, taking the letter from the envelope and starting to read.

I'm propped up on a pillow with nothing better to do than to push my cuticles back with a thumbnail. I'm just on the point of giving him a nudge and telling him he's too poky for words, but something about the intent way he's reading his letter stops me.

A certain stiffening of his shoulders, a certain silence gives warning but I can't guess of what.

"Walter?"

But he just goes on reading, his face stony.

"Has something happened?"

He turns his head and stares at me, his face gone white, so white that above his upper lip his skin has turned a milky blue.

Without a word he passes me the paper in his hands and my hand is already trembling as I take it. I know, I think, already, what the letter is going to say. When I look down it takes me seconds for the words to become legible, for them to make any sense, and then I see *happy . . . total honesty . . . only way that works* . . . But the signature at the bottom of the page, the letters as rounded as a child's, would have been enough.

I lift my eyes, horrified, to Walter's, and he looks back horrified into mine.

"Lee?"

I open my mouth and my lips remain like that, half open. There's nothing I can say.

"You and Victor?" he says. "Oh, god . . ."

His face looks as dazed as a poleaxed calf just before it falls.

"Walter," I say desperately, "I never meant to hurt . . . look, it wasn't . . . I still love you . . ."

He doesn't seem to hear me. He doubles up, like someone struck with a terrible pain, and I can't even touch him, can't say anything, can't justify myself.

155

"I *trusted* you. You were as close to me as my . . . hand. Lee? You know how much I trusted you and love you . . ."

I do, yes, I do. It's only now, though, when it's too late, that I see how terrible my betrayal is. We can never be babes-in-the-woods again, holding hands against the dangers of the night. The horrors and dangers have slipped in the door when we weren't looking and will now occupy the bed between us.

Walter goes to the bathroom. I can hear him in there running water, crying? But all I can do is walk up and down saying his name at the door crack.

I watch, anxious and fearful, for him to come out but when he does he simply brushes past me, his face set. His eyes don't even skim over me and this is, if anything, even worse than the other.

When he gets to the bedroom he goes to the closet and takes a tie from the tie rack and puts it on; then he takes his jacket from the closet and shakes it out.

I stand by the bed uncertain what I should do. "Are you going out?" I ask him finally. "Are you going to the party?" I can hardly believe that he is. How awful to be at the party, holding drinks in our hands, smiling, making conversation about children, movies, schools. That's unthinkable. But to stay here alone, together, is also unthinkable.

When Walter goes down the stairs I hurry behind him. "Walter . . . listen . . ." But my voice is ineffectual, of no more consequence than the sounds a fly makes, nudging the window-pane. "Walter . . . to tell you the truth I thought you knew. Or guessed. We've never been any good at keeping secrets . . ."

But he won't answer, won't say anything. Only once, as we stand by the closet pulling on our coats, he says one thing. "Don't touch me."

So we stand three feet apart to pull on our boots. When we wind mufflers around our necks we look in different parts of the hall, when we pull on our gloves our elbows don't touch.

Outside the snow is still falling heavily and Walter staggers through the drifts. Nevertheless, he walks fast, so fast it is hard for me to keep up and more than once he seems to merge into the whiteness; he is nearly wiped from my sight. I'm afraid to call out to him since I think that he will ignore me, will have become oblivious of my existence. Rage would be better; even tears would be better. But he only hurries on, faster and faster until he's nearly trotting, but whether he is frantic to reach or only to get away, I don't know.

I am still half a block from the house when Walter ascends the Stacks' steps and shakes snow from his hat. By the time I reach the entrance hall which is thick with boots, he has already disappeared, thrown himself into the throng to escape me.

The only person I want to see is Victor since he is the only one I can talk to, the only one, I think, who can be any comfort or help.

Everybody I know seems to be in these rooms — even Fassbinder is in a corner, leaning against the wall on one elbow laughing with a colleague of his about whatever it is that analysts find amusing. But the one person I want to see, the one face I would like to pick out of the throng, seems not to be here.

I have searched through two rooms, have reached the kitchen, when it occurs to me that Victor must be snowed in at the farmhouse and won't be coming to the party. The thought is intolerable; my heart sinks like a stone. I can't endure this evening without Victor. He must be here, in these rooms somewhere, or I will slide behind one of the sofas in despair; I will have a breakdown; I will die.

But then, in the den, in the last possible room, I see him standing by the bookcase. I could nearly sob with relief as I hurry over to him. He is even alone, casting his eyes over the titles of books, and though there are other people in the room I am past caring about them or about what they may think. I put my hand on his shoulder, barely restrain myself from bursting into tears. "Something terrible has happened," I tell him, though he can surely see at a glance that this is true.

He takes my elbow and guides me quickly to the hallway, the little hallway where, months ago, I put my face against his vest and told him I wanted to be dead.

He looks at me solicitiously, hands me his drink which I finish though it doesn't make me feel any better or different, and I tell him the story of my evening.

157

He makes sympathetic noises, guides me to the shadows at the back of the staircase where we are at least half hidden. When I finish talking he puts his arms around me and smooths my hair under his hands. I feel agitation and pain pass back and forth between us like an electric current, but though we stand like that for a long time we don't seem to have anything to say. "Lee?" Victor says finally. "I don't want to lose you."

But we can't continue. He knows it. I know it.

"How could Kate be so stupid," he says, obviously relieved to find something to take out his frustration and anger on.

"If it hadn't been Kate it would only have been someone else."

The recounting of my evening has suddenly made me even more depressed; less agitated, but more depressed. I realize, once I've told him, that Victor can't help. What can he do or say? It is, ultimately, between Walter and me as, in fact, it always has been. "You said we couldn't keep a secret like that for long. I was the one who went on like a stupid child."

"But I did too. I suppose we can always ignore what we don't want to know. But now . . . what can we do?"

But there is really not a thing that Victor can do except to stand where he is at the moment, keeping us both in the shadows for a few minutes.

"Should I talk to Walter do you think? Would that do any good?"

"The day you found Olivia's note would you have wanted to talk to Paolo?"

Victor shakes his head. "No, no, I see what you mean. Impossible."

"I'll let you know. If there's anything to be done . . ."

We kiss, our lips touching chastely for a moment, and then we move out of the shadows.

"Lee," Victor says, squeezing my hand, and I know what he's thinking, what he is hoping for, but though I squeeze his hand back I have to pull mine free.

I must find Walter, must see if he has relented. Because, if he hasn't, how can we endure the night together? How can we bear the emptiness, the averted look, the silence — all as cruel, as implacable as a death in the family?

More calmly than before, but with the same urgency, I pass again through den, kitchen, dining room. Walter is taller than Victor, his red hair should show up easily, but he is not in any of the rooms I pass through. I go through the living room and come out at the hall again where I have the presence of mind to check for boots. But there they are, sitting side by side — black rubber with a button at the top — ugly but serviceable. If there were any doubt at all I turn back the top of one and see *MacDougal* written there in red ink. Walter has always been so careful; he has thought of so many details, that it seems doubly cruel that he should be devastated by the one possibility he never thought he had to consider.

As I bend over the boots I remember coats. Even if Walter left the house so upset he forgot his boots, surely he could not forget his coat. Not on a night like this. So I hurry up the stairs to the Stacks' master bedroom where the coats lie in a great mound on the bed. It's so huge it could conceal lovers, a body, anything. I paw through wildly, taking no notice of the combs and Kleenex that fall from pockets, but before I reach the bottom I find it, Walter's coat, his gloves and scarf stuffed into the pockets. So he must be in the house somewhere, perhaps shut up in a bathroom.

I am halfway across the Persian rug, heading for the door, when I suddenly stop where I am, aware that there is something unusual, something incongruous, although, as I let my eyes wander over the room, I can't see what this could be.

And then I hear it again. There is someone in the room breathing deeply, surely asleep.

At first I think that it is some guest, overcome with drink, who has found some convenient spot in the bedroom to take a nap. But there's no one under the coats, no one under the bed nor behind the drapes.

Where? I stand still, listening, and my eye goes to the sliding door of the closet, a closet big enough to conceal a horse.

When I slide the door open the sound of breathing becomes louder, though I still can't see who's making it. I shove the furs and the dresses around on the hangers before I kneel down to try to see

159

behind the racks of shoes. It becomes apparent to me, in this position, that whoever is breathing in the closet is, indeed, back there behind the shoes, and when I pull the coat aside to make a little more light I can see a dim figure in the shadows. I give a little scream and drop the hem of the coat. No matter how irrational the notion, it seems to me that the figure behind the shoe racks is an animal of some sort, a bear possibly, who has taken refuge from the storm and gone into hiberation in the darkest and most secluded place he could find in the house.

However, a moment's reflection allows me to see how unlikely it is that the breathing could be coming from a bear, nor has it altered in volume or rhythm since I opened the closet door. So, taking courage, I carefully lift the hem of the fur coat once more and pull it aside.

Now, with the light from the bedroom penetrating beyond the racks of shoes, I see the figure back there clearly enough for identification, though the moment I do I draw back and slide the door shut, my heart pounding. My first impulse is to conceal the body, to get rid of the evidence. It is, I suppose, a terrible admission to make that when I first see Walter lying in the Stacks' closet behind the shoes — lying with his knees nearly touching his chin — in the position fetuses are forced to take in their cramped space — that my first thought is fear at being landed with the blame.

But I can't just pretend to have seen nothing, to go back downstairs to sip Scotch and water and talk about summer vacations, so I gently slide the door open once more and call softly into the darkness, "Walter? Is that you back there?"

No answer.

I open the door wider, pull the racks of shoes into the room, and crawl beside him. "Walter?" I say again, shaking his shoulder.

But he seems to have gone into a kind of hiberation after all since he doesn't stir, gives no evidence of having heard.

I don't know what else to do. I lie down beside him, our knees touching. It's our old familiar babes-in-the-woods huddle only this time mine is the only hand stretching across the distance separating us. Walter has his hands tucked under his chin so all I can do is to put mine on his cheek.

I feel sad lying there beside Walter who reminds me a lot of the way the girls look asleep; for awhile he's just removed himself, has sunk inside himself to a space no bigger than a small seed. And yet it's restful, too, lying there with him. Now that he's gone into that hiberation, or whatever it is, he can't look at me with loathing, and whether or not he can hear me, or is listening, I can say to him whatever I want to.

"I think it all goes back to the evening I was born, when Olson grabbed my skinny foot in his hand and squeezed until I cried. That's what I really think."

Walter doesn't disagree, though he doesn't agree, either.

We lie very peacefully together like that for awhile, and then I go downstairs to find Fassbinder.

When Fassbinder bends down and looks at Walter behind the dresses he has a depressed look on his face, like a farmer watching a horde of locusts chew up his corn, but he doesn't seem to consider the matter hopeless. He does not, in fact, even seem very surprised. For him, hiberations in the backs of clothes closets are probably old hat.

16

On Christmas Eve, when the girls and I go to pick up Nina, the airport is teeming with people. I wouldn't have thought it possible that so many people would be trying to either reach Hanover or to get away from it on this crucial day.

The girls are wild with excitement though everything that's going on must seem mysterious to them. They haven't seen Nina for over a year and even Isabel's memory of her is dim — just as last Christmas, with its treats and pleasures, must lie dim in both their memories.

"Will Granny know us?" Isabel asks, her hand straining in mine like a bird struggling to be set free.

"We send her pictures so she knows what you look like. She'd know you anyway, even without pictures, for that matter. One look at your face and she'd know. Will you recognize her, do you think?"

"She's big . . ." Isabel says doubtfully. "Isn't she? And she gave me my farm."

"Yes she did. And she is tall. Nearly as tall as Daddy but her hair's dark."

When Nina's plane lands and I see her descending the steps I cry "Look! There she is!" but Isabel begins chewing on her bottom lip and Felicity puts her thumb in her mouth.

To my eyes, though, Nina is unmistakeable. Only Nina, of all the people I know, would be wearing what looks like a rug over her shoulders and, in a New York winter, sandals with thick soles. Her smile, I see with a pang, is just like Walter's.

I urge the girls to run ahead, to go and meet their grandmother, but they stand back, holding to my coat, and their timidity infects me, too.

But when Nina reaches us, and opens her arms wide, I go into them and hug her as tightly as she does me. "I'm so glad you're here!" I tell her, realizing only at that moment how true it is. How did I get along so long without her?

She manages to press my cheek against the scratchy wool of her serape and pull the girls to her at the same time.

"Oh, look at that!" she says. "Such big girls. And you, Lee, you've gotten thin as a bird."

But we will be all right now, or that is the impression Nina gives us. Everything will be all right, now that she's come. Isabel and Felicity, suddenly knowing this too, grab her hands; by the time we reach the reclaim luggage they are trying to scramble up her legs. Of course the girls have found it hard to be in a household containing, all of a sudden, only one grown-up, only one to give them food and bedtime stories and to try to provide a little diversion in their day. The girls, though, have accepted Walter's absence better than I thought they would. Every morning Isabel asks if Daddy is coming home that day, but when I tell her no, not today but one day soon, she accepts that answer. Two times already she's asked me what he will bring her when he comes. I tell her that whatever it is it will be something nice — something small, I hasten to add — but something she'll like. She just nods her head when I say this as though her thoughts are elsewhere; even very small children know, sometimes, when they shouldn't press a point too far.

As we walk to the car Nina looks sympathetically into my face, takes my hand and squeezes it. "Much better this than if he were run over by a truck," she says comfortingly. "Lot's of things are worse. And who hasn't felt the need for a little rest from the world? I know I have and I'll bet you have too. So don't worry. Walter will be all right."

That night, after we've put the girls to bed, filled their stockings, and I have gone to bed myself, feeling miserable, Nina knocks on the door and comes in bringing mugs of hot milk and honey.

"I knew it," she says triumphantly. "I knew you were in here wide awake and feeling sorry for yourself."

I sit up in bed and turn on the light. Nina has let her hair down and it lies over her shoulders giving her a young, girlish look, though there is a lot of gray in her hair now I see with sorrow.

"Walter always made Ovaltine," I say, tears coming to my eyes.

"Oh, he always did like that terrible stuff," Nina says, scooting my legs over so she can sit on the edge of the bed. "Hot milk and honey is much better. Wards off colds, too."

I take a sip of hot milk, but can't go on with it. "I feel so awful," I say, sliding down in bed and pulling the pillow over my head. "It's all my fault about Walter, Nina. I've done something terrible . . ."

Nina makes angry little clucking noises like a setting hen disturbed from a nest. "We only do what we have to do, neither more nor less, so it's mere self-indulgence to take the blame for everything that happens. Move over and let me come in bed with you so I can keep my feet warm, at least."

"But it's true!" I wail under the pillow.

"Not another word," Nina says. "If you talk like that I just won't listen. Life's too short for that kind of carrying-on. Now, would you like me to tell you a story? Yes or no. About the Christmases I remember when I was a girl."

"That's just like Walter!" I say, starting to cry again. "We were always telling stories to each other."

"In some ways Walter's still just a big boy," Nina says sensibly. "Very sweet, but there's a lot he doesn't know. Here. I'll tell you about the time Uncle Hugh allowed the cat to get drunk, drinking from the eggnog sitting out on the sideboard. Ever hear that one?"

No, I never have. And don't hear much of it this time either because as soon as I get warm I start sliding into sleep. Nina is as satisfying to sleep with as a warm loaf of bread.

Sometime in the night the girls come into bed with us, excitement having made them restless. I wake only enough to let them snuggle in between us, though I know, even in my sleep, that Felicity's toes are digging into my side and her hand is lying on my pillow.

In the morning there we all are—a bedful of women. I'm only sorry that my mother can't climb in too, she's the only one missing, but Nina will have to fill in for her. The mother is the mother is the mother is the mother, after all.

The girls burrow down under the covers, down to our feet, pretending to be rabbits, perhaps, or moles. Something, anyway, that emerges from dark tunnels into the light. They put their faces out of the covers, and wriggle back down again. Only when I've had enough and tell them they're going to have to come out, now, and stay out, do they finally emerge, feet first, swimming backwards, and run down the stairs to get their stockings.

17

Dr. Fassbinder and I stand side by side watching Walter come toward us down the hallway. My heart is beating rapidly, and I'm afraid to look at Walter's face. But I see that his hair has grown long, the way I like it, and his coat hides whatever weight he has put on.

Just in front of us he comes to a stop and sets down his suitcases.

We embrace carefully, kissing each other on the cheeks. There is, unmistakeably, a distance between us so that for me it's like kissing a mannequin. I can't tell what Walter thinks. I don't even know if he still considers himself dead, but decide that Dr. Fassbinder wouldn't let him go home if he still thought that.

"You're looking fine," I tell him. He says that I'm looking fine too. Dr. Fassbinder smiles and seems to approve of the scene. If there's anything wrong with it he doesn't seem to know.

"Well," Walter says, holding his hand out to Dr. Fassbinder to shake. "Thank you for everything."

Dr. Fassbinder beams. He looks truly pleased and I see that he considers Walter a success. In fact, he claps Walter on the shoulder like a father sending a son out into the world.

As Walter and I walk off down the hallway together there is no sound except our footsteps and the light creak of the suitcase handles in Walter's hands.

We both clear our throats at the same moment. "The girls . . .?"

"Oh fine, fine. They can't wait to see you."

"Mother?"

"Oh she's fine too. Just fine. She's been a big help."

Something about the shape of Walter's face doesn't look

right. Was his jaw always as broad as that? It gives me a panicky feeling not to be sure what Walter looked like before. I can't tell if he's changed in looks or if that's only my imagination. The only thing I can be sure about are his clothes. I'd know that coat anywhere and also those brown Hush Puppies with the toes that have worn slick.

But maybe I'm being too sensitive, looking for trouble where there is none. There's always a little bit of awkwardness when you haven't seen a person for a time. People never do look quite the way you'd remembered.

"They fed us pretty well. Have I gained weight do you think?"

"Only a little," I say diplomatically.

"Seems strange . . ." Walter says as we emerge into feeble February sunlight.

"What does?" I ask eagerly, hoping he is going to explain himself to me.

But all he says is, "Well, I have been here for two months so naturally it seems odd to be leaving."

When we get to the car Walter says he wants to show me what he's taking back to the girls. So he opens one of the suitcases and pulls out two flaming red cloth lobsters. They have goggily eyes that roll and have large pincers—undoubtedly two of the most hideous toys I've ever seen in my life. I'd think they'd send a small child into screams.

"What do you think?"

I tell Walter that the girls will like anything he brings them, but I'm by no means sure that this is so. How could the girls give their hearts to those strange lobsters with their silly eyes and grabbing claws?

Yet they do. Or seems to. As soon as Walter opens his suitcase at home and takes out these ugly toys the girls grab them and hug them to their chests as though red lobsters with pincers were the very things they had pined for all their lives.

I can't believe it and look closely at the girls' faces. I'm just sure that, young as they are, they've already learned to disassemble. Some kind of deception is afoot, I'm positive, but who is deceiving whom? Perhaps everything is just the way it seems to be and I'm the one deceived.

I dread going to bed that night. What will Walter and I say to each other when the door is shut, the light is out?

Walter is a long time putting the girls to bed. They must show him their new toys, the new, matching sweaters that Nina has knitted for them. They must have all their old favorite stories read.

I'm already in bed, then, before Walter comes. I have a book in front of my face, but when Walter takes off his dressing gown and slides between the sheets, I lower it and put it across my stomach with the spine bent.

Will we talk? And if we do, what will we talk about?

Walter slides between the sheets, sighs, stretches his toes. "Oh, it's good to be back in my own bed."

Then, remembering something else, he stretches across the bed, leaning on one elbow, and kisses me goodnight. "Goodnight, darling," he says, and goes back to his own side of the bed.

I look at him in surprise, waiting for something more, the old ritual in order to keep the danger away. *I love you and I love you too.*

But this is all Walter says.

When he turns out the light he remains on his side of the bed and I remain on mine, the space in the middle a no-man's-land occupied by neither.

Now that uncertainty lies no further away than the space between our two pillows, then it is everywhere, like air. We can no longer be the innocents, holding hands in the dark woods, making a kind of magic circle to hold the dangers at bay. The dark wood has invaded the magic circle—the dangers and temptations of the world have broken through.

In the morning when I wake up I realize that I have listened all through the night for a sound that I never heard. My sleep was deep, and undisturbed by Walter padding through the house, guarding the barricades. He, too, it appears, can sleep heavily now that the guard has become useless.

I wait for days for Walter to begin talking about what lies between us — to take our old, familiar comfort of putting into words. But Walter doesn't speak of the two months he's been away. He doesn't attempt to fill the gap which, I gradually see, will remain between us; our lives will flow around it like a stream taking a diversion around a rock too big to encompass. No need to say that things will never be the same again. Of course they won't. Things never are the same no matter how many times we may resurrect them in different forms.

Now, at night, after we eat and the girls are in bed, Walter goes to the library to do research on the book about the Hudson River School of American painters that he will write. I go up to the third floor to my study and write during the long quiet hours of the night while the house settles and creaks around me. Somehow I've achieved distance. From this high place near the top of the fir trees I have, or so it seems to me, a kind of godlike vision of all that takes place in the lower regions. I am as high up there as the gymnasium roof and can climb every night to that perilous height, can make that scary ascent. Of course there is the danger of falling. That can always happen. There is no ascent, no ascent whatsoever without danger.

And no ascent without its share of pleasure, either. Even joy.

Up there, in the dead of night, while the snow falls and the wind blows around the chimney with an eery sound, undigested time is returned to me. I finally get to taste the last delicious morsel of that tart eaten so long ago on Lake Maggiore. Whatever it was I lost, when I was ten, in the ratty little woods across the road from our house, I have taken back again, as I have taken from Victor whatever it was I had to have from him — have taken it into myself as he once took the vision of the Baptistry doors. And once inside, it's not likely to be dislodged again.